THE FASTER I WALK, THE SMALLER I AM

THE FASTER I WALK

THE SMALLER I AM

KJERSTI A. SKOMSVOLD

translated by KERRI A. PIERCE

Dalkey Archive Press
Champaign – Dublin – London

Originally published in Norwegian as *Jo Fortere Jeg Går, Jo Mindre Er Jeg*
by Forlaget Oktober A/S, 2009

Copyright © 2009 by Forlaget Oktober A/S
Translation copyright © 2011 by Kerri A. Pierce

Library of Congress Cataloging-in-Publication Data

Skomsvold, Kjersti A., 1979-
[Jo fortere jeg går, jo mindre er jeg. English]
The faster I walk, the smaller I am / Kjersti A. Skomsvold ; translated by Kerri A.
Pierce. -- 1st ed.
p. cm.
"Originally published in Norwegian as Jo Fortere Jeg Går, Jo Mindre Er Jeg by For-
laget Oktober A/S, 2009."
ISBN 978-1-56478-702-6 (hbk. : alk. paper)
I. Pierce, Kerri A. II. Title.
PT8952.29.K65J613 2011
839.82'38--dc23
                          2011019092

Partially funded by the University of Illinois at Urbana-Champaign,
the Norwegian Ministry of Foreign Affairs,
and by a grant from the Illinois Arts Council, a state agency

This translation has been published with the financial support of NORLA

www.dalkeyarchive.com

Cover design by Richard McGuire
Printed on permanent/durable acid-free paper and bound
in the United States of America

For Espen, Åsmund, Mamma, and Pappa

> Ɛ

I LIKE IT WHEN I can be done with something. Like a knitted earwarmer, like winter, spring, summer, fall. Even like Epsilon's career. I like to get things over with. But impatience has consequences. That time when Epsilon gave me an orchid for my birthday. I didn't really want an orchid. I never got the point of flowers, they're just going to wither and die. What I actually wanted was for Epsilon to retire.

"But I need a refuge, away from all the . . ."—for a second I thought he was going to say "togetherness," but instead he said "nakedness." "Does that mean me?" I asked. "I'm not naming any names," he said.

So I undressed for the orchid instead, and soon the buds began to blossom, little pink flowers were springing out everywhere. "I wish you had the same effect on me," Epsilon said.

The directions that came with the orchid said to prune the flowers after they wilt, then they'd revive in six months. First, though, the flowers had to die. So I watched and waited and finally I couldn't stand it any longer. Time to be done, I told myself, and then I pruned the plant down to its skinny, bare stalks.

"What happened here?" Epsilon asked when he came home from work. "I did what I had to do," I said. "The flowers wouldn't wither. But don't worry. There will be flowers again in six months, just in time for fall. If I'd waited any longer, we would have risked not having flowers until winter."

But fall came and went, and then winter, and then spring, the flowers didn't return, the orchid was dead, and for my next birthday I got a throw pillow.

Now that I'm lying in bed, I'm the very opposite of impatient. I'm wishing I could save what little I have left of my life until I know exactly what to do with it. For that to happen I'd have to lock myself in a freezer, but all we've got is the small one in the refrigerator. I can hear people coming home from work, they're thinking about their dinners, and here I am in bed, and the whole thing reminds me of a book I once read.

Maybe I should turn off the lights. Not that it matters, the man with the scythe can see in the dark, he'll find me no matter what. What will it be? My legs? My arms? I'm wondering.

I wiggle my fingers and toes. The left side of my body's numb. The right side too. It'll probably be my heart. Before Epsilon, my heart was like a grape, and now it's like a raisin. Or maybe my shriveled tonsils? You can't trust those things.

It may take a long time before anyone realizes I've died. I read about a Chinese man who was dead in his apartment for twenty years, they could tell from the date on the newspaper on the kitchen table, and when they found him he was just a skeleton in pajamas. I'll wind up a skeleton in pajamas too. But, I'll start to smell before that, and first the neighbors will think it's the Pakistanis on the first floor, but when the Pakistanis start complaining too, someone will remember the little old lady on the third floor. "But didn't she get shot dead during the war?" they'll ask. "No," June, my next-door neighbor, will tell them. "I saw her last Christmas. Time to call emergency."

When I was a child, I always dreamed of being taken away by an ambulance, and when there was one nearby, I'd cross my fingers and whisper: "Let it be me, let it be me," but it never was me, the ambulances were always moving away from me, I could tell by the sirens. Now I hear ambulance sirens in the distance again, they should be coming to get me because I'm wearing clean underwear and will be dying soon. But no, there's someone else in the ambulance instead, someone who's no longer responsible for their own destiny.

It's getting dark, I'm trying to concentrate on something useful, and the only thing that matters now is to figure out what my last words will be. "The probability that we're going to die is smaller than ε, if ε equals a microscopically small quantity," I told Epsilon. It wasn't like me to say something like that. I wish I'd said something different.

I want to say something meaningful, make my last words rhyme, so I lay awake the whole night trying to think up something appropriate. I know I'll never get out of bed again. But then morning comes and I feel so hungry.

Epsilon says that, statistically speaking, a given person will probably die in bed.

Maybe I should get up now.

LIVE LIFE. Seize the day. I'm standing next to my bed, but I don't know how to seize my day. Finally, I decide to do what I always do: read the obituaries.

But first I head for the bathroom. I'm still wearing the black dress from the day before, and from many days before that. Yesterday my dress was especially black. Epsilon is a short man, so I don't know why the bathroom mirror is hung so high. Epsilon says he's happy with it because he just needs to see where to part his hair. My back's so bent I can't see anything. I stretch myself and then putter up to the counter on the tips of my toes. Now I can see the upper half of my face in the mirror, like a nixie lurking with half its head sticking out of water, to lure you in. It's strange to think the half-face in the mirror is me. I look straight into my eyes.

Why bother with appearances when no one's looking? I go out into the hall to get the newspaper.

It's possible that my next-door neighbors, June and his mother, know I exist. Even if they do, they won't miss me when I'm gone. They're the only ones besides Epsilon and me who've lived here since the building was first put up, and I remember June from when he was a little boy. His real name is Rune, but his mother can't pronounce the letter *r*. It was probably his father who came up with the name because he had a special interest in old languages. Later, he got interested in accountants. June's mother is one of the few people I've ever been in the habit of greeting regularly. This was back when we first moved in and I didn't know any better. "Hello," I'd say every time we passed in the hall. And since we passed each other several times a day, the routine got awkward pretty quickly. In the morning it was fine, but then we might see each other when she was coming up from the cellar and I was appearing out of the blue. "Hello." A couple of hours would go by and then we might run into each other outside the laundry room. Each time, I'd say "how are you?" and force myself to smile. When I took garbage to the chute at night and she was hovering around on some mysterious errand, I'd pretend I had bad night vision and couldn't see her. I'd feel my way along the wall in the dimly lit hallway, and the next morning the whole painful routine would start again. It was a relief when her husband left her for the accountant on the floor below and she stopped going out. June was still a kid, and suddenly he was forced to run all the household errands himself, so maybe it isn't surprising that he grew into an unlikable adult. He never said hello when he saw Epsilon and me, and I didn't say hello either. So after the deaf woman moved out of the apartment building, I left all other greetings to Epsilon. "Morning," Epsilon would say and June would ignore him, except the one time he gave us the finger. "How fun," Epsilon said. He wasn't trying to be ironic, Epsilon is never ironic. "That's a new one. Probably something he picked up in the Boy Scouts."

Sometimes June or his mother peeks out their door at the very moment I do, to grab their newspaper off the mat, and it's uncomfortable every time.

I sit down at the kitchen table with my toast. I open the newspaper at random pages until I'm surprised by what I'm looking for. Whenever I buy a bun at the bakery, I always eat the custard in the middle first, and I approach a newspaper in the same way. The list of bankruptcies are like the coconut and the obituaries are the creamy filling. Today I'm glad my name isn't there. Still, an obituary would be proof of my existence, and I wonder if I should send in my own obituary and tell the newspaper to hold on to it and print it when the time is right. I used to read the obituaries to gloat over all the people I'd outlived, but now I don't think it matters, we all live for just a moment anyway.

We'll keep you in our secret hearts, and hold you there so tight, You'll dwell in loving memory, a dearly cherished light.

Wouldn't it be nice if someone remembered how pretty and smart and funny I was, maybe if I'd had children they would've inherited my talents, whatever those are, and my wisdom could've been passed on to the next generation: "Remember to exhale gently in order to puff out your lips when you're being photographed, my dear daughter." But nature only cares about preserving and perpetuating the species, it couldn't care less about individuals, and the fact is that nature actually prefers for individuals to live as briefly as possible, so that new generations can take over faster and evolution can speed up, which is an advantage in the struggle for existence.

"The laws of nature are in direct conflict with our individual interests," Epsilon said. "Isn't that what I've always told you?" I asked him. Ever since Stein died, Epsilon had his nose buried in a book. "What are you reading?" I asked. "I'm reading what Schopenhauer has to say about death," Epsilon said. "I'm trying to make peace with the fact that Stein's gone." "But you're religious," I said. "No, I'm not," Epsilon said. "Oh. So you're hoping to find some other, enduring meaning for Stein?" I asked. Epsilon nodded. "Something like that." "Does Schopenhauer have anything useful to say?" I asked. "Well, the part where he says that Stein will continue on as an expression of the world's will seems a bit much," Epsilon said, "but the thought that he'll live on in the species of Dog, there may be something to that." "So if I imagine a dog in a garden a thousand years ago, standing there eating grass as though this is the solution to all its problems, and then a dog standing there eating grass today, it would in a way be the same dog? That's not as comforting as you might think. Stein was Stein, after all." "Schopenhauer claims you have to overcome the idea of Stein as an individual," Epsilon said, "you have to start identifying him with the totality, because as a part of the totality he'll live on as Dog for a very long time."

Perhaps I should stop seeing myself as an individual and start identifying myself with the totality, but I just can't do that, I'm about as far away from the totality as you can get. But maybe it's not too late. I let myself imagine that someone might notice me on the way to the store. But what would I do if that happened, probably nothing, and whoever it is might be disappointed by what they see. I've never heard of anyone being impressed by nothing, after all, and I don't like to disappoint people.

I have to look through the peephole for a long time before I go out. But I'm not complaining. It's worse for those who have monocles because their vision is going. I wait until all the neighbors on my floor and the floors above have gone out, and the outer door on the first floor has closed a few times, and then I can go out too. I don't shop on the weekends, when too many people are out and about, and Epsilon is at home. I creep down the stairway, then hurry past the neighbors' doors and mailboxes. One time my name was on a mail-order catalogue and I almost bought "the hilarious, one-of-a-kind plastic moose head that sings when you move, guaranteed to make you laugh for years and years to come." But Epsilon prevented it.

When I step outside, I force myself to look up. Nice sun, I think, before looking down at the trash blowing around in the gutter. It's been a month since the superintendent's obituary appeared in the newspaper.

"He died an unnatural death," I said. "Sorry to hear that," Epsilon said, but he seemed more upset that that stubborn zipper on his jacket was stuck. "He should still be glad that he reached the average life span," I said.

But now I'm not so sure. I'm not sure of anything anymore. The courtyard of our building is a mess, and even though I've seen a lot of things in my time, I'm still surprised to find a half-eaten cupcake in a hedge.

There are two young mothers with baby carriages sitting on the grass in front of the building, and even though I'm staring at the asphalt less than usual today, they don't notice me, which is probably just as well, since I saw on TV that people don't say "hello" anymore, but instead ask "what's up?" and I just wouldn't feel comfortable with that.

I follow the sidewalk past the large strip of grass between the buildings and then turn onto the gravel path leading between a line of trees, where the Østmarka forest ends, and then there's just fifty meters or so until I come out on the other side. After that, I walk along the hill past the church, which looks more like a swimming hall, and head for the grocery store. I'm walking pretty fast, but I don't sweat anymore these days.

There's a senior center over the bridge behind the grocery store, but I pretend it's a motorcycle club or a dance hall or something I wouldn't care about anyway. I took dance lessons when I was twelve. Everyone wanted to dance with the lovely Ellisiv, the other kids lined up and took turns. And sometimes, when they least expected it, she'd tip her wheelchair back a little to startle them. I always danced alone. For half an hour I'd be the girl and for the other half hour I'd be the boy.

It's cooler inside the grocery store than it is outside. They've only just opened. Actually, I prefer it when there are other customers in here, so I don't attract attention. I usually buy what other people buy, it's nice to have boiled cod for dinner if the woman in front of me at the checkout is also having boiled cod. "We're not the only ones eating cod today," I say to Epsilon, knowing he appreciates this.

I pick a few apples from the fruit display. Ever since Chernobyl, I always peel Epsilon's apples so his brain won't be affected by any trace of radioactivity. My own apples I just buff on my skirt. I find the cheese, Epsilon likes brown gjetost. I prefer strawberry jam, but jam jars are impossible to open. And when it comes to jars, Epsilon is no help at all. I also like pickles. Then I realize that I could ask an employee to open the jar for me, and I could just screw the lid back on lightly for the trip home, and so I find the jam aisle. There they are: jar upon jar, stretching from floor to ceiling, and even when I put my hands on my hips and lean back, I can't see to the top of the shelf. They all look like they have a screw lid, though, so I just pick one at random.

I'm frustrated because both of the store's employees are standing at their checkout counters, and I'm the only customer in the store. I don't want either of them to feel that I've rejected them. But neither one seems to notice me, so I choose the boy. The girl is probably here just to fill a legal quota, from the looks of her. I put my groceries on the counter and the boy keeps talking to the girl as he scans them. He picks up the jam and beeps it across, but I don't have the courage to ask him to open it. He doesn't tell me how much it costs, but I can see the number on the screen. When I give him my money, I touch the palm of his hand, but he doesn't notice. I brought a net bag with me, I won't ask him for one of the grocery bags under the counter or wonder what else he's keeping down there. I just pack my groceries into my bag and go. And if I was kidnapped five minutes later, and the cops came by and showed him my picture, the boy would say he'd never seen me before in his life.

The hill near the church is hard to climb, and as I pass along the line of trees I'm not as happy as I should be to see the green grass on either side of the path. And suddenly, behind some bushes, I spot a pair of legs. I stop. Right there, right on the path in front of me is a man wearing pants that are a little too short. I get the feeling he's been waiting for me. Perhaps he's from the nursing home next to the church.

He reminds me of a man I saw on our lawn last summer. It was during that tropical heat wave and he looked like a windshield wiper as he bent over the sprinkler trying to get a drink. I want to turn around, but that would be too obvious, what if he gets offended? There's only one thing to do—keep walking, pretend everything's normal. I try to whistle, to show how unaffected I am by his presence, but I only push out air, not music, it's like I'm trying to blow out a candle. When I'm only a couple of meters away, he looks right at me and I stop puffing, but keep on walking. "Excuse me," he says, "do you have the time?" He says this like it's the most natural thing in the world, and perhaps it is, but I know nothing about the time. My watch is up in the attic along with the almanac from my last year in school. "It's half past nine," I say as I pass him, my legs keep moving along. "Thank you," he says. "No, thank you," I say and the whole thing is over in seconds.

My heart is beating so fast, it feels like it's ten meters in front of me, I just had a conversation, I just contributed to society, the stranger trusted me to give him the right time, and time is not to be taken lightly. "Time is everything," I say aloud.

I'm running after my heart all the way home, the young mothers are still sitting on the grass, not paying attention to me, but that's all right because I'm not really thinking about them either.

In the apartment, I put the groceries in the refrigerator. Then I sit in a chair and knit a pair of earwarmers in a complicated zigzag pattern while I try to picture the man's head. Plato's theory of forms must be wrong, because I can't imagine that head-shape more perfect than it was in real life. After I've done three rows, I go into the kitchen and take out the jar of jam. Even though I try as hard as I can, I still can't open it. I try warm water, cold water, rubber gloves, I stick a knife under the edge, and finally I try breaking the glass with a can opener.

I eat bread and gjetost for breakfast and lunch, and then I spend the whole afternoon and evening in front of the TV, just like I always do. Einar Lunde is the news anchor today, he's dressed in burgundy, it clashes with his rosy complexion. He looks as stoic as ever, though, and I wonder if he doesn't know that he's going to die. *Heavy the grief, great the loss, but greater still the gratitude.*

IT'S AN EXAGGERATION to say I'm waking up because I think I never fell asleep, and if I fell asleep, I dreamed that I was awake and couldn't sleep.

Epsilon always sleeps without moving. Before I get up, I usually lay awake with my eyes closed and try to guess whether he's still beside me or not. Today I leave the room with my eyes closed.

I've lived longer than all the *tired limbs* and *busy hands* of the people in today's obituaries, even though I haven't done as much as any of them. I've hardly been outside; and maybe I haven't had a full life. Perhaps I'd feel better if I'd tried to make the world a better place. Or if I'd traveled around the globe. I could've seen Sweden. Or Germany. Of course, what they did during the war wasn't very nice, but I'm not one for holding grudges, and I could've sat at a café in Hamburg and flirted with a waiter: "Ich könnte dich auf-fressen, Reinhart," and didn't H. C. Anderson say that *to travel is to live*?

I think he also said *action is all that gives life meaning*, and today I've decided I'll wear Epsilon's wristwatch, I'm sure he won't mind. "All you'll be needing now is your internal clock," I said when he came home on the day he retired, "just like a migratory bird." Epsilon didn't seem thrilled by this idea, but he took his watch off, and now it's in the drawer of his nightstand. My hands shake as I pick it up. I fasten it on my left wrist, and I feel my back bending even more than usual, my arm weighs a ton, and so does my head. Ep-silon is always careful to keep the watch wound, but now it's stopped and it's off by a week. So I wind it again. If I were brave enough to use the telephone, I'd call the lady at the Time of Day service, but I don't have the courage, and besides, I don't know how much I like her, really, she's a little too presumptuous, so I set the time by "gefühlen." There's a chance that more people will ask me for the time, and I, who have never accomplished much, will be the new Miss Time of Day. Instead of Miss Nothing to Say.

But when I get outdoors no one asks me the time, so in-stead I imagine I'd be a greater success as the new Christopher Hansteen: climbing to the top of the building on Wednesdays and Sundays to hoist a two-colored cylinder up a flagpole. Then, when the clock strikes twelve, I'll lower it so that boats in the harbor and people with telescopes or those in the city can set their watches by it.

I go to the store now and then, and occasionally to the library or around the play school. The good thing about the library is that, if it looks like someone's going to talk to me, I can put my finger over my lips and hush them. Sometimes I do that at the play school too. I've never had to do it at the store. And not really at those other places either. There's nothing to do at the library but read. If I find a book with an appealing cover, I'll go ahead and read the last few pages, sometimes more, and that way I can tell Epsilon that I was there. "It's good for you to get food for the mind," he says. But he seldom appreciates my quotations. "When we hate a human being, we hate what, in him, reminds us of ourselves," I said when he complained that I left the cupboard open all the time. "What isn't in ourselves doesn't upset us." "I always close the cupboard," Epsilon said. "But the door to your heart's open wide," I said. "That's true," Epsilon said.

One of the last verses in the Bible says: "I warn everyone who hears the words of the prophecy of this book: If anyone adds anything to them, God will add to him the plagues described in this book." I was rather surprised to turn the page and find more words.

Outside the play school, I sit on a bench and listen to the children over the fence, behind me. They taught me to say "homo" and I taught them to say "floozy," although they weren't listening. I sit there until a cat finds me, a cat always finds me.

When I get to the jam aisle, I choose another jar—a different brand this time. Hopefully it'll be easier to open. When I try it, though, the lid stays stuck. I set my mind on asking the boy at the register to open it, but change my mind before I've finished the thought. I'm silent and spineless again; even though I was able to speak up once yesterday, I can't rest on laurels like that for very long. Twenty-four hours at most. *Every joyful hour in life is paid for with strife.* Despite the depressing sentiment, at least this one rhymes.

They say old people go looking for pigeons and cats, but the opposite is true. Pigeons and cats come looking for you. "Coo, coo," say the pigeons in front of the store, they walk right up to me, and I answer in a small, accusatory voice: "You-took-my-egg-you, you-took-my-egg-you," which is what we learned in school the wild doves say. When I do that, the pigeons always scatter at once. What's *her kind* doing here? they think. If a cat comes, though, I'm the one who has to scat. One time a big Siamese followed me all the way to the Tveita buildings. Epsilon went pale when I told him the story, because Tveita reminds him of communism and bad taste and everything else that can go wrong. It's hard to know what his politics are; he was more reluctant to go to Tveita with me after someone wrote "anarchy or chaos" in big black letters on the hot-dog stand out front. He used to call me a little bohemian—that was when I was going out to the store barefoot and weaving rugs.

"I could join the Socialist Party," I said. "I suppose you could," he said. "I read in a brochure that membership doesn't cost much a year," I said. "You just have to check the box that says 'low income.' Maybe I can even get a tax deduction for it." "Except you don't pay taxes," Epsilon said. "And now I'm grateful," I said, "because if I did, it would seem cynical to join." "True, true," Epsilon said. "Like all socialists, I would be the sweet and naïve type," I said, "Unless I'm the exception that proves the rule." Epsilon looked confused; again we had both fallen off the train of thought.

On my way home, I climb the hill next to the church. Up ahead, a man is shuffling along with a walker. I bet he can't open jam jars either, but he probably has the courage to ask for help. It's just me who doesn't have the courage, and I could say that it's pride, if I had anything to be proud of. Then I have a good idea: isn't it true that putting other people down makes you feel better? And so I decide I'll make it to the top of the hill before this bag of bones in front of me. If I win, I might have a reason to be proud.

My legs move as quickly as drumsticks, it turns out I can sweat after all, and I use words that I didn't even know I knew. I'm actually a racewalker, and I want my footsteps to be so fast that the human eye can't make them out. I get closer and closer to the old man and then I pass him. Passing people isn't great for community-building, but it feels good, and I'm walking so fast that I nearly don't notice the man behind the bushes, I jump when he's suddenly there asking me the time. I collect myself and lift my heavy left arm, which I have to support with my right hand.

"It's still half past nine," I say, and remain standing there. I'm a soldier at her post, my unsteady limbs are rooted to the ground. Maybe he'll need me for something else. I can't put a single coherent thought together and I'm afraid anything I say will ruin the moment. I whistle a bit and try to ignore the banana he's holding in one hand. I even manage a few real notes this time and smile cautiously, but he doesn't smile back. He just says "well then" and turns and disappears into the trees. *A little angel came down, said hello, and turned around.*

That's what I do too.

As I'm unlocking my apartment door, the neighbor's door opens and June comes out. He stares at me without saying anything.

"You must have it really rough," he says.

I don't know what to say, what can I say?

I can't open the jar of jam and so I eat five slices of plain bread. What's the point of spreading something on bread, anyway?

"Do you remember when we took the bus to the mountains and picked berries? A silly idea, when you think about it," I said. Epsilon and I were eating soup, strange that it was such a short time ago. "Berry picking was a great tradition in my family," Epsilon said, as he had so many times before. Perhaps he blamed me for putting a stop to it. "My mother was best at it," he said. I never met Epsilon's mother, but I can picture her clearly. "I followed you to the very back of the bus," I said, "and then we waited for the bus driver, who was still loading the bags." "I was looking forward to a vacation," Epsilon said, "I was exhausted." "When you put your head on my shoulder, I thought you were asleep," I said, "and I felt quite serene. But then the bus next to us started and you jumped up and shouted, 'We're rolling, we're rolling!'" "I thought our bus was rolling backwards," Epsilon said. "The other passengers were giving you strange looks," I said. "A few were laughing," Epsilon said. "But luckily they soon got over it," I said. "Except for that one guy," Epsilon said, "who just sat and stared." "It was weird," I said. "But you asked him to stop," Epsilon said, "and that wasn't like you, I was surprised." "Me too," I said, "my heart was pounding for a long time." Epsilon smiled at me across the table. "Your gums are a healthy color," I said. I thought that boded well for the future.

I look out the kitchen window at the apartments in the building next door. It's strange to imagine all those people living out their lives, completely unaware that Epsilon and I exist, and so what's the point of having neighbors anyway? They walk around their apartments and act like they're not going to die, but they're going to die, the cashiers at the grocery store are going to die, and the old man with the walker is quite likely already dead now. *You've earned your heavenly sleep, though our earthly sorrow's deep.*

I CAN BE A LOT OF FUN. I remember a joke I once made up: "Have you heard about the man who was so thin his pajamas just had one stripe?" I asked Epsilon. "Yes," Epsilon said. "Impossible," I said, "I just made him up." "No, I'm sure I've heard of him before, Mathea," Epsilon said. "Oh, yeah, you're right," I said. "Come to think of it, I remember a whole article about him in that senior citizens' magazine *Over Sixty*." Typical, you think up a good joke and it turns out you've heard it before. But I laugh anyway, and I tell Epsilon that I'm the funniest person I know. "You don't know anyone besides me," he says. "But still," I say.

How sad it is for the world to have missed out on lively Mathea. But it's sadder for me. So I'm sad for a moment, but then I decide to bury a time capsule. I push back the covers, haul my legs out of bed, and put my feet into Epsilon's worn felt slippers. Then I walk into the kitchen and look under the sink. Back behind the buckets and rags is an old cardboard box that used to hold bottles of detergent. Epsilon always buys in bulk, I have no idea why. The box says "Bulk," and I guess that'll have to be my legacy. I plop it on the kitchen table and think about it a while. Finally, though, I decide it won't work. I need to bury something meaningful. I know what I have to do.

Epsilon sat there staring off into the distance, I thought he was calculating probabilities, but then he said: "I'm going to make you a pine box." "But I'm not dead yet," I said. Back then I had no problem joking about death. "Please don't say things like that, Mathea," Epsilon said. I was knitting an ear-warmer with a bumblebee pattern, Epsilon had been having earaches, wet weather was always hard on him. "Trying to make earwarmers that look summery will be hard," I said, "but I'll give it a shot." Unfortunately, we'd had to cut our camping trip short because our clothes and food and gear had gotten soaked, and there was no way to dry everything before the next downpour.

"I'll make a little pine box," Epsilon continued, "and you can put it next to your stuffed chair, which is actually my chair." "But I've used it so much it won't fit you anymore,"

I said. "Anyway," Epsilon said. "You can keep your knitting things in the box, I've already calculated the dimensions in my head." He was gone for hours, he's not very handy and he'd never been to the sawmill before. When I sing that folk song about the sawmill by the sea, he just half hums the refrain. *Oh hovli-ruvli-ravli-rei. Hurrah!* I'd just knitted the last stitch on the earwarmer when he came through the door carrying boards and a hammer and a folding ruler, along with the most expensive miter saw the store sold. "A clever invention," Epsilon said. "This'll make the box nice and smooth." I stared at it for a long time. "It reminds me of something," I said. "What?" Epsilon asked. "I don't know," I said.

At first I stayed out of his way and let him work in peace, out on the balcony. He stood there in his earwarmer just measuring and angling the saw. It didn't look like he was making much progress, though, so I asked if I could help with sawing. He said that would be good, so that he could focus on measuring.

The day before his vacation was over Epsilon finished the box. It couldn't have been nicer. He'd even varnished it and when I opened the lid I saw that he'd burned "To my beloved Mathea" on the bottom. Usually, I only hear him say "I love you" when we've already gone to bed and he thinks I'm asleep, and I say "ich liebe dich von ganzem Herzen" back to him when I think he's asleep, so I blushed when I read the words at the bottom of the box, and Epsilon blushed even more, and neither of us mentioned it again.

It's been an eternity since Epsilon set that box next to my chair so proudly, and I ceremoniously put my knitting things inside it. I wish someone else knew about this.

I take out all the earwarmers—there are probably seventy or more, some of them itty-bitty—and put them in the detergent box. Then I set the empty wooden box on the kitchen table. I'll bury the box and inside will be things that say something about Mathea Martinsen and her life. It makes sense to start with earwarmers. I dig out the light green one, which has a small dark green pocket on it. That's good for Epsilon to use when he goes to the grocery store, he can keep his change in the pocket. And if there's ever a war, it'll also be good camouflage in the woods. It's white on the inside, so Epsilon can turn it inside out in the winter. Then he can use the pocket for gunpowder. I put the earwarmer on the kitchen table beside the box.

I go into the living room and stand on the green wall-to-wall carpeting we bought because we wanted to have the feeling of grass growing inside. I wanted to paint the ceiling blue, but Epsilon said no, then we might as well just go outside.

I've spent a large part of my life in front of the TV, you want to get your money's worth, after all. Still, Einar Lunde won't fit in my time capsule, and that's a good thing.

On the little table beside the sofa I find the deck of cards we use when we play Old Maid. That doesn't happen too often, because I'm impatient and Epsilon is cheap: Epsilon sits too long calculating probabilities before every draw and I refuse to play unless there's something to play for.

Our wedding picture stands on the bookcase. I take it down and wipe the dust from the glass with my hand. I'm not easy to see because the background the photographer used was about the same color (just like a sunset, he assured us) as my dress ("a dream in apricot," according to the ad in the classifieds). I'm gazing up at Epsilon, exhaling gently to puff out my lips, and wonder if he knows what he's getting himself into.

The bookshelf can't hold much more than Epsilon's books. He has every issue of the *Statistical Yearbook* ever published. Except the one from 1880. They're arranged in order and I don't have the heart to take them down. "You know, Mathea," he said a long time ago, but I remember it well, "that when it comes to violent deaths, men have greater or approximately equal chances as women in all the categories, that is, fire, poisoning, drowning, poisonous plants, murder, and so on, but when it comes to falling, women are in the majority." "The penny drops," I said. But Epsilon simply looked at me as if he couldn't believe what he'd just read. Finally, I began to laugh, which is what I usually do when I don't know how someone wants me to react. Epsilon said that it was no laughing matter, it was something I should think hard about.

All the books have to stay on the bookcase unless Epsilon is reading one of them, and even then he doesn't like to see the empty space it leaves behind. Therefore, there's never a yearbook on his nightstand. I keep a Bible on my nightstand, because Epsilon says statistically it's what people are most likely to have on their nightstands and that's reason enough.

We keep our clothes in the bedroom closet and that's where I find my wedding dress. I want to put it in the time capsule. I wonder what will happen to all our things, they'll probably be thrown out and all our memories with them. And I wonder what the deepest lake in the world is.

I looked at my long feet at the other end of me, by the water's edge. My toes stretched toward the sun like hungry children toward the bowl of gruel. My feet had grown faster than any other part of me. They were already full-grown before I started school. Given the size of my head, though, I think this was just a clever trick on nature's part: it kept me from losing my balance. Epsilon was on his stomach next to me, brushing sand off his book and squinting at the words. I looked at the tent, wondering if I should bother to get my knitting things. "If anyone comes by, you'll have to put your clothes on," Epsilon said. "Are you expecting anyone?" I asked. "Hikers could always turn up," Epsilon said. There's a first time for everything, I thought, so I covered myself.

"You remember the time I didn't have eyebrows?" I asked. Epsilon turned the page. "It was hard for us to communicate back then," I continued. Epsilon didn't answer. "I talked about the electricity in the air, and hinted about what was going on between us," I said, "but you thought I meant it literally." I looked from the sun to Epsilon, but he didn't seem to be listening. "Have you heard this before?" I asked. "I was there," Epsilon said. I brushed a ladybug off his ear and continued: "You were so serious when you said that if I was about to be struck by lightning again, I should keep my legs together to prevent an electric charge building up between them." "It's a fact," Epsilon said. "And it never occurred to me that we were talking about anything other than science." "Exactly," I said. "Lots of people think we have eyebrows to keep the sweat out of our eyes, but actually it's so we can communicate with other people. Shall we go and cool off?"

I stood with the Lutvann Lake up to my navel and waited for Epsilon. He tiptoed out, almost sideways, just like a crab. I shook my head.

The kitchen table is filling up and it's getting dark, I've been at this half a night and a whole day and Einar Lunde is ready with the news. Today he's talking about someone who thinks our goal in life should be to leave no trace—neither when camping nor living in general—and I think I could be an honored member of this movement. But something tells me that they don't put up statues, and besides, I've spent the last day and half the night trying to do just the opposite, to leave some traces behind. Here I have a whole kitchen tableful of traces.

I THOUGHT I WAS ASLEEP, but then I remember I've forgotten to check the desk for something worth burying. It might be nice to bury the phone, but think—what if someone calls? What if someone actually calls?

Epsilon only called me once. That was when we'd just bought the telephone and he called from the phone booth right outside the building. "This is a test, tango echo . . . sierra tango, this is a test," I heard him say before he hung up.

I go out into the hallway and sit on the floor in front of the desk. There's a pile of old telephone books in the top drawer. If someone were ever to ask me if I had a hobby, I'd tell them, yes, I'm a collector. The photo album is in the bottom drawer and the stiff pages creak when I open it. Most of the pictures are from before I was born.

Before Epsilon, it wasn't just me, I had a mother and a father and my father's aunt and uncle, and maybe more than that, but no one bothered to tell me about the rest of them. I was eight when the girl next door told me my parents were my biological parents. And then she couldn't resist—she just had to tell me how they went about it.

When my parents died, I lost contact with Great Uncle Hans and Great Aunt Asta. "It was the best thing for all concerned," I said to Epsilon. Hans died a few years later from a long-dormant birth defect, and the week after the funeral Asta died for no apparent reason.

One of the photos in the album isn't stuck down, it falls into my lap, it was taken before anyone ever gave me a thought, not that anyone ever has, particularly. There's my mother and father and Hans and Asta, it's summer and they're all sitting posed in a row in front of a big cherry tree, they're dressed nice and smiling, even my mother. I've always liked that picture, even though I'm not in it, and now it occurs to me—being dead must feel just like being unborn, and that's not so bad. But you would miss out on snowy trees, cold hands under clothes, and oranges on Orange Hill. And not only that—at least I know that after the cherry-tree picture there will be pictures that have me in them. But as I look through the pictures from my childhood, I realize I've never been photographed alone.

In the very back of the album there are a couple of pictures of a dog I used to take care of. "Stig wagging his tail," a childish scrawl says under one. Then there's "Stig having a good time with his bone"—and the last one is of Stig and me: "Stig is the one on the left."

When I'm putting the album back in the drawer I find the big sandwich bag full of teeth, a souvenir from my first and only job.

"I have good news for you," Epsilon said, we hadn't been married for very long. "Are you going to retire?" I asked. "Of course not. I've just started working," Epsilon said, he'd just been hired at the Central Statistics Office. The good news was that his boss needed a cleaning lady for his house, and wouldn't it be nice for me to get out and mingle with people a bit? "But I don't like mingling with people," I said, "I like mingling with you." "Yes, I noticed," Epsilon said. "So you should feel special," I said. Unfortunately, he'd already told his boss yes, and he was sure no one would be at home while I was doing the cleaning, so people wouldn't be a problem. He smiled so contentedly that I didn't want to point out the flaw in his logic. Sometimes you've got to be generous in marriage. It's a matter of give and take.

After I finished all the work at our employer's house, I couldn't resist looking in the cabinets and drawers. The first interesting thing I found looked like a cigar box, but when I opened it I was disappointed because the box was full of teeth, more than I could count—and I tried. There were milk teeth and molars, teeth with and without fillings, gold teeth and wisdom teeth. I've always envied people who have a mouthful of teeth, because I've never been able to go to the dentist, I just know my tongue would get in the way. As a result, my teeth started jumping ship early on. When I was just a girl, I already knew how it would be, and to this day I worry about the state of my teeth when I eat cucumbers and see the crisscrossed bite marks. Out of envy, I took the tooth collection home. I dumped the teeth in a sandwich bag and figured someday I'd find a use for them. Then I hid the bag underneath the photo album in the bottom drawer, Epsilon wouldn't find it because he's never cared about the photo album. "We have to live in the present, Mathea," he says.

Epsilon bought a cake at the bakery to celebrate, but a couple of days later I could tell by the look on his face that something was wrong. I was worried that his boss had discovered that the teeth were missing, but Epsilon didn't say anything about that. He just said that his boss didn't need a cleaning woman after all. "And you'd just gotten going, Mathea," he said. "I'm so sorry." I comforted him as best I could. "Now I have more time to spend with you," I said.

"But I'll be at work," Epsilon said. "Yes, but you'll be in my thoughts," I said. Epsilon stroked my cheek. "I'm the world's best wife," I said.

Epsilon didn't notice my disappointment. Not that I'd expected his boss to throw me a big going-away party, but a thanks for the effort might've been nice.

I wonder if I should put the teeth into my time capsule, DNA is always useful. Then again, it should probably be my own DNA, and though a few of the teeth in the bag are mine, I have no idea which ones. And I don't have enough teeth left in my mouth to sacrifice them for the cause. I don't have much hair left either. That's not something I worry about, though, because every other Russian president has been bald. I figure I can donate a little dead skin. Every person's DNA is unique, and I like the thought that I'm unique, until it hits me that every person in China is just as unique as me.

It takes me another day to collect all the things I'm going to bury, and now I have to wait until it's dark again. I flip on Einar Lunde. He's trimmed his beard, I see, but the little hamsterlike mustache under his nose has a life all its own.

"Don't you want to watch the news with me?" I ask Epsilon. "No, I'm reading," he says and turns a page in one of his statistics yearbooks. "I've got all the information I need right here." "But something might've happened," I say. "Something might've happened?" he asks. "Even the thought upsets you," I say.

Einar Lunde is talking about people who've died, and they manage to go on dying every single hour until the late news comes on. I don't know why people put up with it, we should stage a protest.

I eat again simply because I can, and then I wonder if I should write a note and put it in the time capsule. Surely I can manage something that doesn't sound like a personals ad, though maybe that's exactly what it is. The one thing I can think of, however, is that I am the only Mathea I know, so I write, "I alone am Mathea." When I look at what I've written, I see "I Mathea am alone," and I wonder if Epsilon knows that. I press my finger beneath it to leave some DNA, and just to be thorough I sneeze on the sheet. I believe in dotting my *i*s and crossing my *t*s.

LESS IS MORE, I say to myself, and then I say it again a little louder. After a lot of negotiation with myself, I've finally decided what's going into the time capsule and what I'm going to write in my note. It all ends up being far less than I'd originally planned. I look out the kitchen window, happy that all the windows opposite ours are dark. I'll bury the box exactly in the middle between the buildings so I can find it in case I change my mind and need to dig it up again—which is rather likely—and that way too, I can keep an eye on it from the kitchen window. While I'm standing there planning my next move, I have to close my eyes, I feel warmth growing beneath the lids, and think maybe I should bury myself instead of the capsule. I don't know if it's worth the effort, or if life is worth living, though maybe that's something I won't know until I'm dead, and probably not even then.

I have to wear dark clothes that blend in with the night. That's fine, because I only have two dresses, a black dress and an apricot wedding dress. I take the black.

"You should make yourself a jacket with some color in it," Epsilon says, "you're so handy with those knitting needles. Not that there's anything wrong with a gray jacket and a black dress, of course, but a little color would be nice. What about the plum red you used on my last earwarmer?" But I could never wear plum red. It's more than enough to walk next to Epsilon's earwarmer.

We keep a shovel in the closet. "It's good to keep a shovel in the closet," Epsilon says, "you'll thank me for that shovel some day, I'm sure of that." I had to bury a rabbit once, and I tell Epsilon thanks again as I stand nervously at the peep-hole with the shovel in my hand and the box under my arm. Then I slip out the door and down the stairs. The breeze is cold and refreshing, I draw the night into my lungs and try to calm myself down, it's been a long time since I was out after the nine o'clock news. I stopped going out late after that girl Therese was kidnapped.

Her picture was on the front page, she'd disappeared one day while she was out playing, just up and vanished off the face of the earth. One moment she was on the street in front of her building, the next moment she was gone. I remember the letter her mother wrote to the kidnappers begging them to give her Therese back. The whole affair made me feel a little weird, or maybe that was only menopause.

I was constantly on the lookout. If anyone asked me for directions, I'd run the other way. One time I passed a car parked on our street and got a bad feeling when I noticed that there was only one black leather glove on the dashboard—where was the other one?

I talked Epsilon into buying a rabbit, but didn't tell him it was because I couldn't be alone in the apartment anymore. He wouldn't understand. "I just love animals," I said. "Almost as much as Hitler did."

The very evening we got it, the rabbit started throwing up. I hadn't named it yet, I'd hardly even touched the white ball of fur, so I know it couldn't have been my fault. I had to stay up the whole night watching. When Epsilon woke up, I'd already gone out and buried it. "Where?" Epsilon asked. "I'm not telling you," I said. "I don't want you to go dig it up."

Then we got some fish, but despite their presence, I was scared every time I came home after being at the library. "Hello, Epsilon," I'd say into the stillness, making sure that the kidnappers lurking behind the curtains or the bedroom door could hear me loud and clear. I'd ask, "How was karate today?" then exclaim, "Why Epsilon, you've left your gun lying out again!"

My fear diminished with time and the hot flashes were gone before I knew it. But I never forgot little Therese.

Shovel over my shoulder, I make my way to the center of the yard. I really hope no one can see me. If they can, I'll just tell them I'm picking up trash. I begin to dig. Eventually my arms get so tired I have to stop, but at least I've dug a big enough hole for the box. "Bon voyage," I say and it bothers me that I can't come up with something that rhymes. I refill the hole and then tamp the grass back down on top of it. Luckily, the lawn is ugly enough that I don't think anyone will be able to tell where I've dug, I hope it's not just the darkness deceiving me. After that, I hurry back inside. Out of the corner of my eye, I spy—that rhymes—a flier hanging on the bulletin board, I hardly even knew we had a bulletin board, I'm usually so busy looking at the floor. The words "CLEAN-UP!!!" leap out at me, they force me to take a step back, it shouldn't be necessary to shout like that. I don't have the courage to read the rest of the flier and scurry back up the stairs.

I FEEL THE NEED to scratch my bites until they bleed. That rhymes. Maybe it was the mosquito bites I got outside in the dark, or the adrenaline left over from the burial, or the flier about the gathering that kept me awake all night. I look at my bloody fingertip. Lovely, another sign that I'm alive, and seeing my breath on the kitchen window while checking my teeth too. Thinking that I like the sight of blood scares me though, so I force myself to think about something else. I wipe my fingers on a napkin and look out over the lawn. Unless you were in on the secret, you'd never guess something was buried out there, so I suppose I can breathe easier now. But as far as helping with my state of mind, the box doesn't seem to be working at all. I wonder why, maybe it won't work until someone digs it up again, though by the time that happens I'll probably be six feet under.

I decide to go to the store after breakfast, even though I don't need anything. There's a flier in the entryway advertising a get-together at the senior center, and the thought makes me ill, so I read about the community clean-up instead. I see that it will take place this weekend, but get no farther than that before a sound on the floor above me sends me scurrying out the door.

We've never had a community gathering before. Since the old super did everything himself, there wasn't a point. And now he's dead. Odd that they haven't replaced him. I can't go, that's completely out of the question. Then again, I have a shovel and maybe they'll need someone with a shovel. Plus, I need to make sure no one finds my box. I could bring homemade rolls, my popularity in the building would skyrocket, I'd be adored by one and all, reporters from the Groruddalen papers could snap pictures as my neighbors carry me around the lawn. I've always loved the idea of being carried like that.

I walk through the woods. The only thing that catches my eye is a mushroom, a white destroying angel. It's deadly. At first I'm disappointed that the man with the banana isn't here, but then I tell myself that you can't depend on others for your happiness, you have to make your own happiness, Mathea.

In the store I buy ingredients for dozens of rolls and several batches of meringue, and I buy three different jars of jam too. When I'm in line at the register, I realize that I won't have room for everything in my small net bag and I'll be forced to ask for a grocery bag. Then I remember a news story about how many Swedes are working in Norway now and I don't know the word for "grocery bag" in Swedish. But without asking or even looking at me, the cashier puts two extra bags on the conveyer belt, and I'm so relieved that I whisper "thanks," although I say it in Swedish and it sounds like a sigh.

The bags are heavy and that's a good thing, I'm sore after my night's work, I like being sore, it tells me I've accomplished something. Soreness is probably my favorite feeling. Next to love, of course. Sometimes my tongue gets a little sore, and even though Epsilon always kisses without using his tongue, I always kiss with mine because then I know it's there, the only muscle in the body that's just attached at one end, a fact I don't like to think about. It reminds me of everything I've lost. The kites I flew when I was a child—the string broke every time. The dog I walked, the leash that snapped, I never saw Stig again.

In spite of my soreness, I easily catch up to the people walking ahead of me. When I reach the foyer, I read the entire flier on the message board. "There will be a community gathering next Sunday," it reads. "All residents must attend!!!!" I gulp and read the rest of the flier as quickly as I can, just in case there's something even worse there, but I don't know what could be worse than what I've just read. "Come and give our new caretaker, Leif, a warm communal welcome and help us win back the title of Groruddalen's best co-op!" Oh no, I think, but I can also feel excitement building, I guess I do have to go, I don't want them to toss me out on my ear. But then I read the last line, it says the elderly and disabled are exempt, and I'm both relieved and disappointed. When I get up to the third floor, June is standing in his doorway shaking his head. It seems like he's trying to spook me. I close the door behind me and start to bake.

I always baked buns and rolls, but meringue was my specialty, and Stein ate it all by the truckload until the day he died. I tried to convince Epsilon that he'd committed suicide. "He'd been looking depressed lately," I said. In reality, though, it was me who killed him. He was our substitute child, since no matter how hard we tried, I couldn't get pregnant. At first we thought it was because of our bunk bed.

"Knowing you, you'll want to be on top," Epsilon said. "No," I said, even though I meant yes. So Epsilon climbed unsteadily to the top bunk. He'd been scared of heights ever since he climbed a ladder and discovered that going up is much easier than coming down, which must be because our eyes are closer to our hands than our feet, Epsilon is an extreme example of this. Finally, I realized that I had to put an end to this madness, so I let him descend from above and sleep next to me—but there was just something wrong with me. If I'd known this sooner, it would have spared me a lot of worrying. When the neighbor girl told me that sperm can sneak up inside you and get you pregnant when you least expect it, I was determined that this would never happen to me, so I bathed wearing all the underwear I owned, one pair pulled over the next. Maybe I was so determined not to get pregnant, it was impossible to change my mind later on. So, Epsilon and I got a Dalmatian instead.

We argued back and forth about whether his name would be Black or White. "Why not something a little less racist," I suggested. "We're forward-thinking people. Let's call him King, after Martin Luther King. We can set an example." So we called him King, and that went fine until the first Negro moved to Haugerud. Instead of sniffing the man in passing like he did everyone else, King went crazy. He barked and growled and threw himself at the poor guy. We assumed it was a one-time thing, but then it happened again and again. Apparently our dog was the narrow-minded type, and even though we liked him, we decided we shouldn't call him King, so we named him after Epsilon's uncle. We called him

Stein, which means stone. Appropriate, when you consider the way he died.

It was early fall and Stein and I were walking to Lutvann like always. I had plenty of meringues in my pocket and every once in a while I'd toss him one, since that was the only way you could get him to keep going. Finally, we sat by the water's edge; Stein liked to watch the waves lap at the shore. Epsilon thought Stein must be intelligent since he'd sit and grin whenever Epsilon started in about statistics. At long last, someone who appreciates averages. Stein sat with the same thoughtful smile whenever he watched the water. "There's a lot of math in waves," Epsilon said. That day there wasn't much wind, so I threw stones in the water to give Einstein something to think about, and before we knew it we were surrounded by a school class, dogs are kid magnets. There was nothing to be done, escape was impossible. "Look at the fat dog," a plump kid said, the plump ones are always the loudmouths. "Can it swim?" another asked. I didn't know what to say, Stein had never shown any interest in swimming. The kids laughed and I was embarrassed on Stein's behalf, so I whispered, "Swim, Stein, swim," but he just grinned at me. Time for a meringue. I stuck my hand in my pocket and reached for the little bag. Stein was immediately alert, but the bag was empty. We'll see how smart you really are, I thought, before I took two or three quick steps and made an exaggerated throwing motion toward the water. Stein jumped straight in the water; a couple of children got wet, which was fine with me, and he began to swim. Usually the meringues didn't go too far, because throwing a meringue is like throwing a cotton ball, but maybe he was fooled by my running start, as by now he was ten or twenty meters out. When would he realize that I'd just thrown air? I was worried. "Where's he going?" one little girl asked. Soon all I could see was the white and black head bobbing up and down and then Stein was gone. "He's gone," the fat boy said. The kids looked from the water back to me, and I didn't know what else to do, so I pretended everything was fine.

After a few minutes, the kids turned around and left, but I watched the water until evening came on and the sun went down. Then I walked home and told Epsilon that Stein had left us. "The possibility of that happening must be less than ε, if ε equals a microscopically small quantity," Epsilon said when I told him how it happened.

I bake and wonder how I'm ever going to go to the gathering, because even if I'm not disabled, I'm definitely old, no one will expect to see me there, and one of the worst things you can do is disappoint someone's expectations.

A diligent life has run its course, a busy hand has worked its fill, your long labors are at an end, your loyal heart is finally still.

I don't like lying on my back at night anymore, I feel like a corpse, especially when I put my legs together, which I almost always do, and fold my hands across my chest. The feeling of being in a coffin is uncomfortable, so now I usually lay on my stomach with my legs splayed. I have flexible hips.

Sometimes I go to sleep, but I wake up when the telephone rings. I'm not brave enough to answer it, but Epsilon tells me to answer it, because it might be important. And then I find out it was only a dream.

THE BIG CLEAN-UP is today, my neighbors are standing right over the time capsule, that's nice, it's like I'm there, too, even though it's not really the same thing at all. They're talking and laughing, which is strange, because aren't they there against their will? I figured the mood would be glummer, but apparently some people must enjoy forced labor.

The rolls are on the kitchen counter, I've set out the jam jars, but I can't bring myself to go down. What should I say, here I come with rolls and jam? That just sounds pathetic. Of course, I could claim a little corner of the lawn and pick up trash, there's plenty of that lying around, but what if someone saw me, they wouldn't recognize me and maybe they'd think I was someone from another building complex who'd come to destroy the flowerbeds, so my own complex would look like a better place to live and be known as Groruddalen's best co-op. There aren't a lot of old people there, although some of them definitely look over-the-hill, even more so than me, and anyway it's probably good to have a bent back if you're picking up trash. One man is missing a leg, but he's a real champion with a rake, he hobbles here and there, back and forth, even though he could've stayed at home: "Sorry, I only have one leg." I wish I only had one leg.

The one extraordinary thing I can brag about, though, is that I was struck by lightning once, but can I really brag about that? It was the lightning that struck me, after all, and not the other way around. And because of that, Epsilon saw me for the first time. He must've been born with some superhuman power that made it possible to notice me. The fact that we ended up together is thanks to him rather than me.

Still, I was good at sorting playing cards into their various suits. So I shuffled them—"seven times is the correct number of times to shuffle a deck," Epsilon said, "neither more nor less"—and I was also quick at sorting them by number and color. "You're good at sorting cards," Epsilon said. That warmed me to the bone and I "accidentally" dropped the cards on the floor so I could sort them again. I was also good at starting new rolls of toilet paper, I could unstick the first sheet without tearing it. "Epsilon," I'd call out when I knew it was time to begin a new roll. "Are you done on the toilet?" Then I'd go in and start a new roll, voilà! perfection, before tearing off seven sheets for him, the statistically correct number, neither more nor less.

When Epsilon was at work and I was alone in the house, I didn't do much of anything. I didn't have any children to watch and I only cleaned superficially. Every once in a while I'd wash my eyes out with a shot glass of water, but now that I think about it, I didn't do nearly enough, and nothing mattered anyway.

I watch June's mother and all the other neighbors working outside, and I wish I were under house arrest. Trapped in my home, like Aung San Suu Kyi. I could never set foot out of doors, and all I'd ever see were the walls, floor, and ceiling of my own apartment. There would be nothing I could do about it, my life would never change. The world, though, would demand my freedom. Amnesty International would campaign, people from every country would write letters of protest, they'd hold demonstrations and chant rhyming slogans: "Let there be no doubt, we want Mathea out," with special emphasis on the rhyming words. But nothing would work, and wouldn't it be nice to have an excuse.

They're setting out the hot dogs now. It's strange that hot dogs are still so popular after all these years, I remember Uncle Hans coming home from America with a hot dog in a bun, he meant it as a warning. Imagine how embarrassing it would've been to show up with rolls and jam, they're probably out of style.

I catch sight of the man who must be the new super, his T-shirt says "Caretaker Leif," but I suppose he could simply be an admirer. He has a hot dog in one hand and a tiny girl in the other, and if he let go of her he'd never find her again. He stands talking to his new neighbors while the girl tugs at his arm to get his attention. When he finally turns to her, his eyes wander over the building, and suddenly he's looking right at me on the third floor. I immediately dodge behind the curtains. This is just how it felt the time I was struck by lightning, it's like my eyebrows are burning off all over again. I don't dare look back, what if he's still looking at my window and wondering if he should invite me down to have a hot dog, I hardly remember how to eat them, much less how to digest those long monsters. What am I going to do if he rings the doorbell? I'll just have to act like I'm asleep. If I hear him trying to pick the lock, I'll make snoring sounds and hopefully he won't think something's wrong with me. "She's resting," Leif will say, "we'd better just let her sleep, she can have leftovers tomorrow."

I stand by the window and peek through the gap between the wall and the curtain until evening is well underway, but no one comes to try to pick my lock. My neighbors disappear from the lawn at the same rate that rolls disappear from the kitchen counter; when darkness falls, both places are empty. I take a bite of the last roll. Oh dear, I think, when I see the bite marks.

IN THE NEWSPAPER I read an article by a doctor jabbering away, and he mentions "memento mori," which might be what I've contracted. Is there a cure? But then I'd have to go to the doctor, and I can't bring myself to do it. I've been there before.

Epsilon and I were taking a walk one Sunday, I was tired and confused by what he was saying, but he just wouldn't stop. "Hush," I managed to say before the lump in my throat got too big. Epsilon looked at me. "I thought I heard a cuckoo," I said. Epsilon listened, but after a few seconds of blessed silence he resumed the subject. Finally, I couldn't take it any longer, and pulled my arm away from him. The path of least resistance is my preferred distance, I thought. That rhymes. Then I ran as fast as I could down the hill. Epsilon was still at the top, probably babbling on about all the obstacles June's mother had overcome. My legs could barely keep up with the rest of my body. Still, something was holding me back, I didn't know what it was, but I knew what Epsilon would say. "It's common sense. What did I tell you about women and falling, Mathea?" I picked up speed and left common sense behind. This is how it feels to run as fast as you can, I thought, right before I ended up with my face in the gravel.

I could hear ambulance sirens, but they were going the wrong way. Then again, I could hear Epsilon coming closer and closer, and I didn't need an ambulance as long as I had him. "Matheamathea," he said, "your leg—it's perpendicular to your torso, we have to call an ambulance." "No-no, I'm fine," I said and looked up. "Let's not make a fuss." "But you have to go to the emergency room and let them put your hip back into place," Epsilon said. "No need, everything's fine," I said and smiled to reassure him, but then a tooth fell out. "You're not thinking straight," Epsilon said. "I'm going to call a taxi."

When we got to the emergency room, I tried to walk in without help, I didn't want to be a bother, but a nurse forced me onto a stretcher. "I'll make sure you're first in line, you must be in so much pain," she said. "No, I hardly feel a thing," I said. "Don't give it a thought." "Sometimes I just can't figure you out," Epsilon said.

The waiting room was packed and everyone was staring at me. I regretted that I hadn't cut to the front of the line, but then the door opened and everyone turned their attention to the next unlucky patient. It was an old man, and he looked so sad that Epsilon's lower lip began to tremble. "What can we do for you?" the nurse at the desk asked. "I need to talk to a doctor," the man said, his voice so low the entire waiting room had to lean forward to hear him. "I need to talk to a doctor because there's a smell outside my house and I'm scared there's some drug addicts hanging around, I heard on the news that drug smoke smells sweet." "But are you hurt?" the nurse asked. "No, not at all," the man said in a trembling voice, "but I need to talk to a doctor." The nurse and the other people in the waiting room had no idea why the man needed to talk to the doctor, and Epsilon and I were likewise in the dark. But now I understand.

For a long time after my tumble on the hill, Epsilon had to take over all the housework, since I was supposed to keep my right hip completely still. So Epsilon cooked and served dinner, while I lay on the sofa with my throw pillow. I realized that I needed to give something back, so I started a correspondence course in German. I figured it would be good for us both.

"Komm mal hier, Liebling," I said when he took off his earwarmer and hung it on the hook in the hall. But I don't think he understood what I said, because he immediately began vacuuming. "Ich will mit Ihnen nicht Schindluder treiben," I said quietly, but the whir of the vacuum drowned me out.

It's evening and I'm watching the news and eating my cucumber. Einar Lunde is talking to a meteorologist who says that a storm named Leif is on its way, and then he says that that the next storm will have a woman's name that starts with the letter *M*. I realize there's a chance Mathea will be put on the weather map, and then Caretaker Leif and I will have something in common, we can compete when we meet, arguing over whose storm moves the quickest.

The weather report is over, the meteorologist bids me good night, I say thank you while I gnaw on my cucumber and think about the bite marks. I'm thinking about them because Descartes says *I think, therefore I am.* But to my horror one of my incisors tumbles out and last night I lost a tiny mole, it was on the sheet when I woke up, there's getting to be less and less of me. Where will it end?

The tooth is stuck in the cucumber, I taste blood in my mouth and stare in some confusion at what now looks like the sort of weapon you'd kill a seal with. I work the tooth loose and try to stick it back in its hole, but it's outgrown it, it's like it's gotten a taste of the big city and won't go home again: "I feel too confined there."

None of the teeth in the sandwich bag fit either. With or without roots—I try them all, growing more and more desperate with each failed attempt. "Just like the square root of minus one," Epsilon says. "There's no possible solution."

EPSILON GRABBED HIS BRIEFCASE and headed for the door, I asked him why, but he didn't answer. "Should I quit asking?" I asked. "You should quit waiting, Mathea," he said. I often wanted to call the Central Statistics Office: "He's way over the age of retirement." But I couldn't bring myself to do it.

I'm finally listening to the dial tone, it reminds me of a hymn I learned in school, and then the doorbell rings. At first I think it's Epsilon, but I know it won't be him. I freeze and the doorbell rings again. I hang up the telephone and peek out the peephole. It's not Epsilon. It's June.

"I know you're in there," I hear him say.

How do you know that? I think.

"I see your eyeball in the peephole," he says.

"Ditto," I whisper back. I've actually wondered if it's possible to peep through peepholes from the outside to see if anyone's spying on you from the inside, since I like to pretend my neighbors watch what I do all day: "We need to keep our eye on the old woman on the third floor, that way when she dies she won't start to stink, just imagine, the smell might seep into the walls, that would affect the value of the whole building," and I've tried to see if I could make out their pupils in their own peepholes as I pass by, but I've never been able to settle the matter one way or the other. It's impossible to conduct the experiment on your own door all by yourself, I've tried.

"Having trouble deciding to open up?" June asks when I open the door.

"No," I say, "I was on the telephone."

"I see," he says, as though he doesn't believe me. "Well, can I borrow some sugar?"

Before I have time to answer, he hands me a cup that reads "Oslo." I take it and head for the kitchen. Luckily, I still have some sugar left from the baking I did for the community gathering, otherwise I would've had to get to the store without June noticing, it would be too embarrassing to admit I didn't have any sugar, everyone has sugar. I fill the cup and when I come out of the kitchen there's a surprise waiting for me, because he's standing there in the living room. A human being is actually standing on our carpet. I don't know what I should say or do, but after a little consideration, I say "here you go" and hand him the cup. He takes it without looking at me. I expect him to thank me and leave, but instead he asks me if I have a problem with moisture in the walls.

"We've never had a problem with moisture," he continues. "But then again, you never know. What about your bathroom, do you have problems with moisture there?"

He's looking at me now and surely he expects an answer.

"Sometimes I shower," I say. "But usually I just splash a little water on my armpits." It's surprisingly easy to talk, probably because I know I'm his intellectual superior.

He looks at me without understanding. Then he turns his attention to the living-room walls. He raps them with his knuckles. After that, he runs his hand back and forth over the wallpaper before climbing on the chair that stands next to the sideboard. Then he takes some masking tape from his back pocket and begins to run it along the molding, he can manage a meter and a half before he has to move the chair again, and it's like that the whole way around the room. He takes all the pictures off the wall and leans them against the coffee table, and then he takes out a paintbrush. He spackles over the fork marks. Then he rips up the carpet and lays parquet. He tosses Epsilon's chair and my TV into a skip he's rented, it's standing outside the building and every time some neighbor sees the chance to get rid of some ratty bamboo blinds or an old beat-up sofa, he gets mad and tells them to rent their own dumpster. Soon there's not a millimeter of my and Epsilon's life left, it's only June and his things and his smell and his friends, he tells them how terrible the place used to look, and his mother, she brings him dinner every day at five o'clock, even Sundays, and takes his dirty clothes down as soon as the laundry room is free.

He's inspecting the living room up and down and back and forth. "If we were to tear down the wall between our apartments, we'd have the biggest king-size apartment in all of Haugerud," he says and laughs.

I laugh softly too, so it won't get awkward. When you're as old as me, you should know better than to laugh with idiots just to be polite, but I don't know any better, I'm almost a hundred, just a stone's throw away, but acting like I was born yesterday. That sort of rhymes.

June turns and leaves the apartment without saying goodbye, his head filled with decorating ideas.

I watch TV for a long time without really looking at it, all I can think about are his hands on my wallpaper and his feet on my carpet and his laughing, but then the news begins and maybe Einar Lunde will say something comforting. It's nice to know that everything could be much worse,

I could've been blown to pieces by a bomb, but instead I'm just old and incontinent, and I just have that bladder problem when I laugh, which I don't really remember how to do anymore. But instead of Einar Lunde, Jon Gelius is tonight's news anchor. That's a disappointment, I thought he'd been fired. I'm still hoping he'll cheer me up, but then he starts talking about the first warm day in China. They flash pictures of a beach, there must be a hundred thousand Chinese people there and they're so packed in that only about half of them can lie on the sand. It's obviously meant to be a happy story, because Jon Gelius is smiling with his eyes. However, it just gives me the feeling that we're all so insignificant in the grand scheme of things, I could've been a Chinese person on the beach. We're all Chinese people now, or do I mean we're all Social Democrats? I remember reading somewhere that the total number of people alive on earth today is greater than the total number of people who have died throughout all time, and I wonder when the opposite will be true, when there will be more dead people than living, because if that were the case, then at least I could be helping to tip the scale in favor of the dead. It would be nice to make a difference. As it stands, though, being dead is more special than being alive, and I've sometimes thought that plenty of people get more attention after death than they ever did when they were living. Although in my case, it'll probably be about equal.

I remember when Epsilon's attention was completely focused on the woman in the glittering leotard hanging from a long rope. I have no idea how he'd talked me into going to the circus. I must've been intoxicated. The woman climbed and twirled up and down, up and down. It was nothing compared to what I could do on a bar. Epsilon's ears were flapping my way as usual, so it was easy for him to hear what I said. "Do you smell that stench?" I whispered. "It's the animals," Epsilon whispered back. But as I watched the woman in the leotard, I formed my own opinions. She gyrated on and on, it couldn't possibly have gotten more boring. But then it did. Finally, she did a couple of twirls and landed on the floor. Just to be polite, I gasped.

Today isn't going to get any better. You've had a really bad day, Mathea, so aren't you grateful you don't have many days left, I tell myself—*you were patient in life, now rest from strife*—but then I think of the sound of the humming dial tone, why do I have to be so optimistic by nature, why can't I just lay myself down and die?

"THE CHANCES OF BEING STRUCK by lightning twice in the same spot are less than ε, if ε equals a microscopically small quantity" was the first thing Epsilon said to me. "It's completely unbelievable." He didn't know how truly unbelievable it was, because nothing had ever singled me out. The spun bottle never pointed at me, the neighborhood kids never found me when we played hide-and-seek, and I never found the almond in the pudding at Christmas, one or the other of my parents always found it, which was almost a bit suspicious.

It was a cloudless day, I was standing by myself in a corner of the school yard and trying to look busy counting rocks. You're only fooling yourself if you think you can't be lonely just because you're busy, but the most important thing is that no one else thinks you're lonely. While I was standing there, dark clouds suddenly rushed in, the heavens opened up, and bolts of lightning struck me in the forehead twice. I fell back and everything was dark and very far away, I could hear ambulances and this time I knew they were coming for me. "While you wait," a faceless man said, "I want you to draw a diagram of your life, here's a red pen." So I took the pen and drew a line from one ear to the other, straight across my face, and then I pointed at my nose and said: "This is where I am now." I heard sirens and opened my eyes and saw that the whole school had gathered around me, there was a burnt smell and the principal was there. "I think she's hurt her nose, she's pointing at her nose," he said. Two men in white jackets came into view, they put me on a stretcher and carefully lifted me into the ambulance, as if I was someone they cared about. Then we drove away, sirens blaring, and it was as beautiful as Beethoven's Fifth.

Everyone at the hospital was attentive and kind, the nurses looked at me compassionately and said that it probably wouldn't take too long for my eyebrows to grow back. The other patients were also nice, it seemed like getting struck by lightning earns people's respect, as if we lightning survivors are God's chosen. Kind of like Moses. "You were so lucky," the doctor said, and I felt lucky, I only cried whenever I looked at myself in the mirror and when I had to go home.

During my stay in the hospital, I'd practiced what I would tell the other students, who would surely flock around me when I came back. "I've never experienced anything so painful," I'd say. "The doctor said it's a miracle I survived." They'd all gasp and thank God that I was still alive. I practiced hiding my scorched eyebrows with my hands so that it looked natural, either by placing a forefinger over each of them, like the sign language for "ox," or I could pretend I was shading my face from the sun. "I've gotten so popular it's really starting to wear me down," I'd tell my mother and father, who couldn't be more proud.

But when I went back to school, my Moses complex had disappeared, because the news on everyone's lips was that the crown prince was back from London after the war. During first period, the teacher forgot to call my name, like always, but instead of saying "Mathea—here" to myself like I usually did, I raised my hand. "Excuse me," I said, "but I've returned." The lightning had apparently given me a positively charged dose of self-confidence. The teacher lifted his eyes from the attendance list that lay in front of him on his desk, the other students turned around and stared at me where I sat in the back row, and I laid my hands over my scorched eyebrows and pretended I was shading my face from all the attention. The teacher had to think a minute, but finally he remembered me: "Oh, we thought . . ." Then he didn't say anything more, and everyone turned back around towards the blackboard, and during recess I was alone counting rocks again.

I'd reached one hundred and seventy-seven when I saw two big ears coming my way from across the schoolyard, it was the skinny boy they called "trophy cup." He was in the same grade as me, and I knew I was the one he was heading toward, because I was alone within a radius of twenty meters, I was always alone within a range of twenty meters, sometimes more. He walked with determination, as though he was afraid he'd change his mind if he hesitated. I got nervous and started counting rocks faster and faster, and I tried to look surprised when he stopped beside me and cleared his throat like he was about to give a speech. "The chance of being struck by lightning twice on the same spot must be less than ε, if ε equals a microscopically small quantity," he said with a serious expression on his face. I didn't know what to say, so I didn't say anything at first, but then I remembered my missing eyebrows, so I made the sign of the ox. I mooed so that it would seem more natural. He had innocent eyes, and I knew he wasn't the type who tears the legs off spiders or cuts earthworms in two to see if the parts will become two new ones. "I wondered how you were doing, and I'm relieved to see you on your feet again," he said. "And you know, you look good without eyebrows, it makes your face so open." At first I was embarrassed, but then I realized this was the first time someone had lied to me to make me feel better. "Thank you," I said and dropped my hands. "I think you look good with big ears too," I said. "Well," he said, "they're not so bad, it's just unfortunate they get cold so easily." "Yes, that's unfortunate," I said. "But in any case," he said, "if you don't mind, and if it's not too hard on you, I'd like to hear what it was like to be struck by lightning, and I can even show you some probability calculations I've done about your experience, it really is unbelievable." "I'd like that," I said and smiled. He smiled too, then turned to go. He took two steps, hesitated, and then looked back at me. "You know, Mathea," he said, "if you count both big and small ones, there are three hundred and forty-five rocks here. I counted them yesterday."

As soon as we were finished with school, Epsilon got a job and we got married and then it was just Epsilon and me.

"EUREKA," I SAY when I read about exposure therapy in the newspaper, that's obviously what I need. Anne Norunn (37) is terrified of bacteria and gets scared to death when her husband—he's actually younger than her—Kent (35) sneezes. Anne Norunn spends a fortune on soap and detergents and is even considering divorcing Kent, who's a walking time bomb of filth, she'd rather have an air purifier for a husband. "Exposure therapy is what you need," the psychologist says. "You have to gradually expose yourself to bacteria more and more until finally you can be with Kent again." "I don't think that's possible," Anne Norunn says. "But it is," the psychologist says.

I need to expose myself more and more to death—without going too far, it's a delicate balance—but then at last I'll be able to live with the fact that I'm going to die. I figure this can be done in two ways and so I draw up a list.

1. I can visit graveyards, go to funerals, or I can plan my own funeral. When I told Epsilon which song I wanted played at my funeral, I was laughing because I wasn't going to die. I stopped laughing when he took out a pencil and wrote it down in his almanac.

It must be terrible to plan your own funeral. It's probably easier to plan other people's.

2. I can begin living dangerously. I can cross the street without first looking left, then right, then left again.

The last possibility I can think of is to "forget" to turn off the hot plate, and I decide to get right on that. In the news, you read about houses and apartments burning down because old people forget to turn off their hot plates, but then again, maybe they don't forget, they "forget."

I switch the hot plate on high and then I sit on a kitchen chair and wait. I wait a long time, but my fear of dying doesn't let up, I just get hot, like Pol Pot. In fact, the whole apartment is getting warm and oppressive, and I'm tired of the green carpet and brown wallpaper, I want to get out, I want to live, I want to go to the salon, but I can't go to the salon, I went there before my wedding and every time the hairdresser dragged a comb through my hair and it hit my ears, I flinched and thought "never again," but I have to get out out out, and I stand up and run out the door without bothering with the peephole, I couldn't care less about the peephole, and I take the stairs in slippers, I throw myself against the heavy outer door and run over the sidewalk to the grass where I lay down.

I go back inside.

There's no one in the foyer. The flier for the community gathering is still up, and so is the one for the get-together at the senior center. I feel sick again. There are a bunch of new fliers too. "Bodil is lost," one says. Bodil is a guinea pig, and there's a picture of Bodil from happier times. The bulletin board is obviously something my neighbors pay attention to, and maybe I should hang a picture of myself with the caption that I've gone missing: "Has anyone seen this old woman? Reward offered. Call Mathea Martinsen." At first I treat the idea like a joke, but then it hits me that it deserves some serious consideration. So I seriously consider it. But then I see Bodil's picture again, and there's no way I can compete with Bodil: those mischievous, marble eyes of hers guarantee that no one will take any notice of me.

I'm about to leave when a black flier with gold lettering catches my eye. "Attention neighbors," it says. Apparently, June is celebrating his birthday. A warning: "There's going to be a party."

Saturday comes, and I'm still annoyed that June is having visitors. Epsilon and I had a visitor once, a cousin neither of us knew we had. One day he just called us up out of the blue and asked if he could stop by. "Of course you can," Epsilon said. "We can hardly wait."

We scoured the apartment from top to bottom, I baked meringue and rolls and then I cut my hair. Using a strip of tape as a guide, I cut my bangs straight across and then diagonally along the sides, and then I trimmed along the edges. "That looks almost too straight," Epsilon said. "It can never be too straight," I said.

We were afraid we wouldn't have anything to say to our cousin, and we spent half the day on the couch brainstorming things to talk about. Worried that he could show up at any time, I didn't dare go to the bathroom, how foolish to be sitting on the toilet when our guest rings the bell. "We should open the door together," Epsilon said, "so we can see which one of us he recognizes." "If he recognizes both of us, at least we can be glad we never had children," I said. Epsilon got quiet and had a strange look on his face. "If we'd had a son, I would've called him Aksel," he said. "That sounds like 'acceleration,'" I said, "and then we wouldn't mind if he was a little slow."

We sprang up when the doorbell rang and then I couldn't hold it any longer. "I have to go to the bathroom," I said. "*Right* now?" Epsilon asked. "What are the odds?" In the bathroom, I found the perfume Epsilon had given to me for my birthday. I'd never used it before, I was afraid it would cause a stir if such an insignificant woman started smelling so strong, but I took a chance and sprayed my body's pulse points, just like it said in the women's magazines—behind the knees, on the groin, on the wrists, on the neck, and behind the ears. I went out again and sat on the sofa with Epsilon and our visitor. "Are you wearing perfume?" Epsilon asked and coughed. I blushed and tried to look surprised. "No, are you?"

We never found out whose cousin he was, but after waiting a week—we didn't want to seem desperate—we called him to ask if he was planning to stop by again. He wasn't. "Did he say why?" I asked Epsilon. "No," Epsilon said. "But I'm sure it had nothing to do with us."

Out the kitchen window I can see that people dressed in party clothes with presents in their hands are making their way into the building, and June has put on some music: "*Hello lamppost, whatcha knowin'? I've come to watch your flowers growin'. Ain't cha got no rhymes for me? Doot-in doo-doo feelin' groovy. I got no deeds to do, no promises to keep. I'm dappled and drowsy and ready to sleep. Let the morning time drop all its petals on me. Life I love you, all is groovy.*"

"AT LEAST I NEVER had to put up with the wrong crowd and peer pressure and smoking and drinking," a pale girl says on TV, a crazy man has kept Natascha prisoner in a little underground cellar nearly her whole life. And it hits me that I could've been an alcoholic. If I'd gotten out more, I definitely would've been. Never mind the wrong crowd I could've fallen in with.

It was unfortunate that the housewives in the building used to get together on Tuesdays, because I was always in a foul mood on Tuesdays. I don't know exactly why, but Epsilon says Tuesday is named for the war god Tyr, and I'm probably a pacifist, so maybe that had something to do with it.

Whenever I got home from one of those get-togethers, I sat down at the kitchen table and wrote to Epsilon. I always made sure that what I wrote ended on a happy note. If I was stuck, I'd pace back and forth until I found a solution, it was tiring, but I always felt better afterward.

Sometimes I wrote about a friend I had when I was little, but that didn't happen often, since it was hard to make "she buried me in anthills" rhyme with anything.

"Mathea can't come out and play today," I said. "Why not?" she asked. "Mathea isn't here," I said. "But you're standing right in front of me," she said. "I am? Where?" I asked and looked around. "Don't be so silly," she said and laughed.

She was two years older than me and always played the priest, I was the corpse. Sometimes there was a funeral procession, but she was the only one who could see it, maybe those thick lenses of hers were made of some special glass that let her see things no one else could. First she anointed me with saliva and then I had to lay on the north side of the tree. Complaining only made it worse, and the one time I tried to get away, she caught me and then declared it would be a cremation rather than a burial.

"They go crazy when we move them from the south side to the north side," she said, pouring a shovelful of ants down on me. "Did you notice that?" "Yes," I said, but I didn't blame them. I shut my mouth and eyes tight and held my breath, and all I could hear was the ants crying inconsolably, and I tried to think of something comforting to tell them.

The first time it happened, I told my father. He said that anthill therapy was good for rheumatic complaints, he'd heard about a man whose back and hip pain was cured after he'd sat in an anthill for a couple of hours.

I'd put what I'd written into envelopes and stick them in Epsilon's briefcase, that way he could read them while he ate his lunch. We never talked about them, Epsilon would just start crying. It was enough to see the understanding in his eyes. And the admiration when I came up with really good rhymes.

Now and then I also wrote to strangers—the unlucky few I'd pick at random from the telephone directory. I'd cut out pictures of food from magazines and newspapers and glue them to pieces of paper: "Only five kroner for a box of dates," I'd write. "Just come to the grocery store at Haugerud." Imagining the look on their faces when they walked up to the register to pay has saved me from depression time and again.

When June's mother began to go to the housewife meetings too, I stopped, and now I say to myself how lucky I was to get out before I gave in to so many bad influences.

The policeman who talked to Natascha after she escaped from Mr. Priklopil's cellar after eight years of captivity said he was astounded by "her intelligence, her vocabulary." I get chills just thinking about it. I also get them when Natascha talks about her escape, how she dashed hundreds of meters between hedges and yards and streets, hopping over fences and begging passersby to call the police. But they just ignored her.

THE DAY I REALIZED I could write things down was the day I first told Epsilon how I felt about him. It was the first winter after the lightning strike, we were always together, but every time I opened my mouth to say what I wanted to say, I got the unbearable urge to stick my tongue against cold metal, that way it would be attached to something at both ends, so I just kept my mouth shut.

One day Epsilon asked if I wanted to sit on the back of his sled. "Where are you going?" I asked. "Where do you want to go?" he asked. "I don't mind," I said. I put my arms around him, his hat smelled like wet wool. Then a girl from his class appeared, she wanted to sled with us. Surprised, Epsilon and I looked up at her. "I don't think there's room," I said, but she'd already sat down. We set off, snow hit my eyes, so I closed them and nudged my face into Epsilon's jacket. When I looked again, we were out over the ice. I asked where his friend was, she wasn't sitting behind me on the sled anymore. We looked up the hill, but she wasn't there either. "Maybe it's a sign," I said. Epsilon took my hands and helped me up, and we stood together with our wet mittens, holding hands. I wanted to tell him how much I cared about him, but instead I told him that last year seven people had been killed by sharks and fourteen by toasters. Epsilon gave me a strange look and I wanted to disappear. "I just have to . . ." I said, without knowing what I actually wanted. I knew what Epsilon thought I had to do, though, because he turned quickly around and left. I blushed standing there and heard his crunching steps on the ice. "I'll make a snowball while I'm waiting," he said loudly, as though I'd worry he'd be peeking at me. I figured it couldn't get any worse, so I began to take off my shoes. After some effort, I was done. "Come and see," I said. My tongue barely obeyed me. But Epsilon stood motionless, and I had to call his name again before he started toward me hesitantly, his eyes fixed on the sky. "Look down," I said when he was close. I got anxious when he lowered his eyes and saw my scarf, which now formed a heart on the ice. Within the heart, my wet mittens and socks formed the letters: *N I*. I wasn't trying to spell "nine," as in the number of lives I had left. It was now or never. "Your real name is longer than it sounds," I said and felt my toes turn blue.

I NEED TO GO to the store and buy sugar in case June comes to "borrow" more. I'd be lying if I said I didn't hope to meet the man without a watch on the way. Before I go, I spray on perfume, but this time I just squirt myself behind the knees. And a few drops behind the ears. And one squirt in the air in front of me as I'm walking.

When I reach the woods, he's there, as if by appointment, and I know that this is the chance I've been waiting for. June's visit gave me the self-confidence I needed, the man on the path obviously isn't quite all there, therefore I can talk to him. Now all I need is something to say. Quickly.

"Hi," I say. It's as if I'm listening to a stranger's voice.

His expression doesn't change.

"Do you think it's nice here?" I ask.

He doesn't answer.

"Yes, it's nice here," I say.

"Yeah," he mumbles. He doesn't say anything else, and I feel panic setting in, he obviously doesn't like small talk. I'm scared he'll disappear again if I don't think of something interesting to say, quickly.

"What's your name?" I ask. I can't believe I have the courage.

With a serious expression, he mumbles something that sounds like "KGB," and I get nervous, because that's the sort of thing that puts you on your guard. But when I ask again, I hear him sigh "Åge B.," and I would sigh too if I was stuck with that name. I don't have the courage to ask what the "B" stands for, in case it's something embarrassing, and so I just nod encouragingly.

"That's a good name for a man," I say.

I'm disappointed that he doesn't ask me what my name is, or what my favorite color is, or which cassette tape I'd take with me to a desert island if I could choose only one. It's so wonderful to talk, I want to talk to Åge B. about everything I talked to Epsilon about. When Epsilon came home from work, I'd ask him how his day had been and what he'd done, and he'd say his day was good and he hadn't done much. I thanked him for this window into his world. Then he'd ask me how my day was and what I'd done, and

I'd tell him some story, like about how I think I saw a baby snake shedding its skin on the bathroom floor, but instead it was just a dust bunny. "Don't you ever get the urge to talk to someone other than me?" Epsilon would ask every now and then. "But I've done that," I'd say. "Don't you remember the time I went with you to the Christmas party?"

"Well then," Åge B. says.

"Well then," I say and hurry off before he does.

I walk down toward the church and feel fat. Especially around the thighs. I hear that's a normal reaction when you get rejected by someone of the opposite sex.

One time I really was fat, it was right after Stein died. I'd stopped walking to the lake, but I hadn't stopped baking meringue, in fact I baked it even more often, and at first I thought that's why my dress was getting tight around the waist. "Don't you think I'm getting a little soft?" I asked Epsilon. But Epsilon didn't want to hurt my feelings and said that on the contrary I was looking quite stiff.

"'Aunt Flow' hasn't visited for a while," I said to Epsilon, I couldn't wait any longer. "She should've been here at least three times now." I usually said "Aunt Flow," so Epsilon wouldn't get embarrassed, and now he took my hands in his. "But does this mean . . . ?" he asked. "I think it means more than we can imagine," I said. I looked at Epsilon and thought this is what true happiness looks like. Even though I'd become immune to the tears in his eyes—I'd seen them often enough—this time they were contagious.

Epsilon went with me to buy a new dress. I had to wear the new one home, since I'd taken the old one off in the dressing room and couldn't get it back on again. I needed something to grow into, so I bought a dress that was so huge I could wear it over my coat. "But is that really necessary?" Epsilon asked. "No," I said. "But it can't hurt." Even though I was walking right beside him, he looked anywhere but at me, like he was trying to figure out where I'd gone. It was probably because the white dress blended with the snow in the gutters. I asked him to pull down the scarf he'd drawn up to his nose, because it hid the lower half of his face. "People will think you're doing drugs."

For the first time, Epsilon didn't ask if I wanted to go with him to the Christmas party. He just put the invitation on the desk and assumed he'd be going alone. So I told him I wanted to come with him. If anyone asked me a question, I could just pat my belly and that would be answer enough. Plus, no matter how awful the experience was, I wouldn't be facing it alone. Now I was a two-for-one. Epsilon called me brave, and I got a sudden whim and knitted a long red belt, which I tied in a huge bow around my waist, red on white. When we arrived at the Statistics Office cafeteria though, I was feeling much less brave, especially when I realized I wouldn't be sitting beside Epsilon at all. "Mrs. Martinsen" read a name card at the other end of the horseshoe-shaped table. Before I could tell him I'd changed my mind and that this was a bad idea, Epsilon was already on the way to his seat. I nervously adjusted my bow and sat down. The chair to my right was empty. On my left was "Mr. Dahl." Luckily, he was drunk. However, he snuffled so much I had no idea what he was saying; in fact, he was only saying one word over and over. I guessed: "Eskimo?" Dahl shook his head and, struggling not to fall out of his seat, said the word again. "Genghis Khan?" I asked. The whole time I was watching Epsilon, wanting him to see what a social butterfly his wife was. Dinner came and went. But then, three more tries: "Geronimo?" I asked at last. "Geronimo!" said Dahl. We were both relieved. However, neither of us had anything to add, and during dessert we just sat there and nodded.

I could see that Epsilon was keyed up, and I could tell that the woman at his table was quite the extrovert. She laughed at something he said, and when she got up from the table and headed for the bathroom, I followed her. I wanted to tell her that Epsilon wasn't funny at all, even though I knew

I'd never be brave enough to say it. However, at least I could make sure she saw my stomach. I acted like I was washing my hands when she came staggering out of the stall. She came up beside me and studied herself in the mirror. She was wearing a simple black dress. I wadded my red belt into a bundle. She began drawing her fingers through her hair, which hung over her shoulders, and said she really should comb it. I didn't know who she was talking to because there was no one else there. I tied the red belt on again. "You have long hair," I said, more to myself than to her. "It's not long enough," she said. Then she closed her eyes, I didn't know why. I thought maybe she was trying to imagine something as she stood there swaying. That made me uncomfortable, because now I was forced to try and imagine what she was imagining, which was her, covered only by her long hair. Then I remembered that her hair wasn't long enough. I left the bathroom before she could open her eyes. Since I felt talked out, I found Epsilon and said I was ready to go. But he said he'd promised the woman at his table a dance. "You're not a funny man," I wanted to say. But then he thoughtfully asked if I was feeling okay, so I told him that on a scale of *one* to *three,* things were fine with me. That rhymed, even though I didn't mean it.

I stood against the wall and watched them. It was hard to stay still. What I really wanted to do was march up to him and say: "I'm putting my foot down, Epsilon." I crossed my arms over my stomach, then dropped them to my sides, and finally I performed a few dance steps. I didn't know what to do with myself. Epsilon looked like a different person. Funnier, now that I thought about it, but in a good way. The hair on the back of his head stuck out just like his ears; the woman's hand nested on the back of his neck. Finally, I calmed down, because I realized that I was only jealous of myself: after all, I was the one who was actually with him. I even loved him.

I spent the rest of Advent in a chair knitting itty-bitty ear-warmers. I could almost see the baby playing on the green rug at my feet, and if the baby wanted to go outside, I could watch from the kitchen window.

But late on Christmas Eve, right before we were about to walk around the Christmas tree, "Aunt Flow" finally turned up, accompanied by an unbearable stomach cramp. I threw the white dress down the garbage chute and stopped baking, and soon my old dress hung from my shoulders and then it swallowed me. It swallowed me more and more, and when our Constitution Day rolled around in May, I was much smaller than Epsilon.

"Smoked ham and scrambled eggs, Mathea." I heard Epsilon put the platter on the night table before he sat down on the chair by the bedside. I opened my eyes. There was a balloon hanging from the ceiling. "I bought it on Karl Johan Street," Epsilon said. "Oh," I said. He was wearing his suit and he sat with his elbows on his knees, hands folded. "Aren't you going to ask?" he said. I didn't know what he meant. Then he said, "You always want to bet on everything. How long do you think it'll stay on the ceiling?" "Epsilon, I'm too tired," I said. There was a breeze coming in from the window. I was cold and pulled the cover up to my chin. "I think it'll last a week," he said. "Or, no, I'm going to say two. What do you think?" "I don't know," I said. "More or less?" he insisted. It felt like I was going to have to contend with that balloon forever. I sighed: "More." "So if I win," said Epsilon, "then you have to have dinner with me in a nice restaurant, and afterward we'll go to the theater." I closed my eyes. "I couldn't." "But that's what I want," Epsilon said. "What do you want if you win?" I didn't answer. "You can think about it," Epsilon said. I turned over on my side, so he wouldn't know that I was crying again. Behind me I heard him spread the napkin on his lap and pick up the silverware.

Neither of us mentioned the balloon again, even though it hovered right over our heads like a speech bubble in a cartoon and I imagined it was full of incomprehensible signs. The day before I was due to win the bet, I finally decided what I wanted. I didn't know how I was going to manage, but I got up and took a knitting needle out of my pine box. The air left the balloon like a sigh of relief. When Epsilon came home from work, I was ready to go out. I'd pinned my hair up with a clip and pinched my cheeks. He stared at me bewildered as I stood in the hall with my shoes on, all ready to go. My coat had gotten so big on me. "You won," I said. A deep sob came from Epsilon's throat, he'd probably held it in for far too long.

I smoothed the wrinkles from his forehead with my fingers. "You look beautiful," he said. "Thank you," I said and glanced down. He kissed my head. I caressed his shoe with the tip of mine." "Did you get new laces?" I asked. "No," Epsilon said. "Oh," I said. And then we began to laugh.

I don't remember the dinner or what we talked about, maybe we didn't talk much. I also don't remember what we saw at the theater. But it doesn't matter.

Even though we had turned a corner, the pain didn't go away, and after that hardly a day went by that Epsilon didn't have some kind of greeting from me in his briefcase.

It's impossible not to notice that the trees in front of the church are budding. Soon it will be Constitution Day again. I remember a small, curious girl who marched with the Lutvann school band. She marched behind the main body of the band, which was playing, and in front of the beginners' band, which trailed silently after. She carried a long, thin poll with a plastic doll on top. The doll was dressed in a brown uniform and had a hat with an orange tassel—a miniature replica of the girl and the rest of the beginners. I don't know why they'd stuck a doll on a pole, what the point of it was, but the girl looked proud as she could be. I imagined her marching over a hilltop, or past the big cars parked on the side of the road, and how she would struggle to hold the doll up as high as she could.

This year I'll march across the palace square and wave to the king. He'll pick me out of the enormous crowd. His guards will come running and take me by the arms: "The king wants to see you on the castle balcony." "What, me?" I'll ask and look up at Harald or Haakon or whatever his name is, and he'll stand and nod. "Yes, you. No one else but you."

I bang my knee hard on the metal edge of a shopping cart. I glance around, but luckily no one's looking. The pain is like a spike in my perfumed knee. I shake my fist at the cart as I go into the store.

Now at least I know his name, I think on the way home. "Åge B. isn't here," I say aloud and it feels totally natural.

"I'LL GET IT," Epsilon said. As usual, though, the Gallup people only wanted to talk to the person in the house with the most recent birthday. "Do you really think that's fair," I asked, "when that person is me fifty out of fifty-two weeks of the year?" Reluctantly, I went to the telephone, there was no good way to get out of it.

I heard a story one time about some rich Americans who, after reading Poe's story about the woman buried alive, demanded that telephones be installed in their coffins, although I could've told them this was a wasted effort, because no one ever calls. I've realized it's up to me, and so I dig the most recent telephone book out of my collection to find "Martinsen." But who am I kidding, I never even made it onto the school attendance lists. On the last day of school, when the principal was handing out the report cards, I stood with the other students as they were called one by one, until finally I was standing alone. "Who are you?" the principal asked.

I imagine my name won't be on my gravestone either. It's a pity, really, because I like my name better and better with every day that passes.

"Mathea Martinsen," I said and held out my hand. The new neighbor proudly folded down the canopy of her baby carriage. "And this is little June," his mother said, beaming at the father. "Oh," I said, "a woman in today's obituaries had the same name."

"Did you notice they all have the same hair color?" I asked Epsilon afterwards. "Could be," Epsilon said. "I really don't think that's necessary," I said.

"Martin Martinsen," I read in the telephone directory. "Mary," "Mary," "Mary," when did Mary get to be so popular? "Mary" and "Mathea Martinsen" are both listed. My eyes begin to well up, because I'm really there after all, so why doesn't anybody ever call? No one ever calls. What's more, my name is listed twice, but the second one has the wrong address, so I can tell it isn't me, and how can someone else be named Mathea Martinsen, I'm Mathea Martinsen. Or, maybe the other woman is the real Mathea Martinsen. That's probably it. Still, I almost feel like I'm a part of the totality, as Schopenhauer described it, and after staring at the asterisk on the bottom left of the telephone, I'm finally able to dial my own number. Luckily, it's busy. I'm a very busy person, "pressed for time" is my middle name.

I've taken an important step in life, and now I have to take one more. You can't stay still because then you'll go into hibernation and before you know it your life has slipped through your fingers. I need to call Information and ask for Mathea Martinsen in Haugerud, maybe Information keeps statistics as to the most requested and most loved person in the nation, a Top Ten Requested Numbers, and I shouldn't just sit here moping around because my name isn't on the list. I should do something about it.

I contemplate the top half of my reflection in the mirror and practice my lines, I ask for Mathea Martinsen in Haugerud: fast and slow, emotional and indifferent, with and without bangs. Finally, I have my lines down.

I speak loud and clear so that my words will reach the person on the other end of the line, they might have to travel a long distance.

"Do you want to be connected?" the man asks.

"No no no!" I shout.

"Oh, okay," the man is as surprised as I am at my outburst. He gives me the number, I write it in the air in front of me, and I ask him to repeat the last few numbers one more time, so as to show off my communication skills.

"Thank you for calling," he says.

"Thank you for answering," I say.

I call and ask for my number until the evening news comes on, and I use a different voice every time. When I die, the operators will ask, mournfully: "Do you remember Mathea, she set the all-time record for number of requests, she was number one on our Top Ten list, do you remember how busy we were back then?"

I accomplished something today, I think to myself as I switch on Einar Lunde. Thankfully, Jon Gelius is out of the picture. I actually accomplished something, I tell myself again, I became someone, you can't sweep Mathea Martinsen under the rug anymore.

Today's guest on the Sunday news is an old woman who's won the King's Gold Medal of Merit. For fifty years, rain or shine, she'd get up at six every morning, put on boots, grab a sweater, and walk to her little shed in the garden to record the weather measurements for the last twenty-four hours, before going back to her house and reporting her findings to the Meteorological Institute. It seems like a very important task, and she keeps a big lock on the little shed in the garden, probably to keep people from tampering with her stuff, otherwise someone on their way home from a bar might pee in her measuring cup and yell, "I've got some yellow rain for you, grandma!" Now she's at the castle receiving her medal, and I'm sitting here and seeing how much she's accomplished. She's even a year younger than I am, and you don't get to be a guest on the Sunday evening news by calling Information and asking for your own telephone number. Suddenly, I realize they might have known it was me asking for my own number. I'm the world's biggest joke, I'll definitely be a joke at the Information office. Einar Lunde smiles at the lady with the medal and I don't know what I should do, all I can do is compensate with another joke, so I choose the one about the pajamas. But no one laughs.

"MATHEA MARTINSEN—*deeply loved, dearly missed*," I write at the top of a page and underline it. "*You were always loving, gentle, and kind, you departed this world before your time, with future achievements waiting in line.*" I draw a thirty-degree angle with Epsilon's protractor. I try to think of something cheerful, like the fact that as a member of the Housing Association I get a ten percent discount on my coffin and gravestone, but that just depresses me more. Surely I can think of something that doesn't involve funerals or hot plates. I take out a new sheet of paper and start writing.

3. Become a Christian. *I am the resurrection and the life. He who believes in Me will live, even though he dies.* One Easter morning I was feeling religious, but then on the evening

news they showed a cupboard full of human skulls. "That's why I don't like watching the news," Epsilon says. "I don't want to risk seeing a cupboard full of human skulls."

4. Pretend I'm a tree. One time I saw Yoko Ono on TV, she had an exhibit: trees growing from coffins. Being a tree must be boring, to just stand there and stare. I'd know: I stand and stare quite a lot. Nonetheless, I decide to walk out into the woods and see what it feels like to be a tree, maybe it's better than I think.

On my way to Lutvann, I see a dog peeing on a pine, I give him a disapproving glare and mumble a few ugly words. I walk on and it feels like my insides are celebrating that I'm back in the woods again. I recognize the roots and stones on the path, the trees stand like they've always done, and it's nice to feel like they've been waiting for me. "You don't look a day older," I say. "You look quite a bit younger," they say, "and your bangs are very cute." Without warning I stumble across an anthill and I gasp a little. But when I raise my eyes, the lake is still there, even though someone once dug a leaky tunnel beneath it, and somewhere out there is a meringue made of air and a stone that couldn't swim.

I walk farther along the water's edge toward the place where Epsilon and I used to camp. Before Stein drowned, we spent our summers here, and now it's nearly summer again.

I sit down on a tree stump and eavesdrop on the conversation taking place above my head.

Not even a little gray bird, which sings amidst the flowers and leaves, will I find on the other side, and this is a thought that grieves. Not even a little gray bird, and never a birch standing white, but on the most beautiful summer day, I have longed for that land of night.

I also talk a little, almost harmonizing with the birdsong. "Do you remember the time you ate lichen after you lost that bet, and you were sick to your stomach for a week?" I ask. "A week?" Epsilon says. "I was sick for months. I don't think I'm over it yet."

For the sake of our health, or more likely because we had nothing better to do, I thought up a morning exercise routine on the beach. I was the teacher, Epsilon was the slow, reluctant student. But sometimes I think he had fun doing it. "It's like riding a horse," he told me when I forced him to do knee bends. He could be an oddball. "That's a clever image, Epsilon," I said. "Thank you."

In the evenings, I tried to talk him into skinny-dipping with me because it sounded romantic, but he refused to follow me into the water after an unfortunate episode with a jellyfish. They can bite, you know, and even though we were far away from both salt water and jellyfish, he didn't want to risk anything. I could only talk him into wading in the nude, and so that's what we did.

Before we went to sleep, Epsilon read to me about standard deviations and confidence intervals and I held the flashlight. Soon both I and the flashlight were out, but I'm sure Epsilon kept reading by the light of the moon, and it feels nice to have someone awake while you're falling asleep.

Epsilon woke me one Sunday morning by saying, "Orienteering. You'd be a natural." I pinched myself in the arm. "But aren't you afraid I'll get hurt?" I asked. In a daze, I sat up against the headboard. "This isn't about me anymore," he said. But it was all about him.

The local athletic club had put up fliers saying that on Midsummer's Day they were going to hold an orienteering race for amateurs. When the day arrived, I stood at the starting line and Epsilon stood on the sidelines with his thumb up, he always did tend to exaggerate. They fired the starting shot and I ran in a near panic from the crowd. I flew over rocks and grass, and checkpoints leaped out at me like distress signals in a fog. Before I knew it, I saw the finishing line and the spectators waiting there to cheer on the winner. I stopped, turned around, and went home.

"I stood there forever," Epsilon said when he came in the door, it was pretty late. "What happened?" He didn't sound the least bit worried. Instead, he sounded irritated. "You tell me," I said from the chair in the living room.

He went into the bathroom to get ready for bed. "Hey!" he shouted. "Who put my toothbrush on the foot scrubber?"

I try to stand up straight and stare while I ponder the conundrum of a tree falling in the forest. If no one hears it, does the tree make a sound, or does it even really fall in the first place? Maybe it would be better for me to be felled with no witnesses. While I chew that thought over, I discover that what I thought was a brown twig next to my foot isn't a twig at all. It's a frog. It sits next to me, motionless, as if it belongs to the plant kingdom, and I'm sure that it, like me, does this because of its fear of death, it's probably trying to keep from being eaten. That's a clever trick: cheat death by becoming invisible.

After the night, the morning, bidding all darkness cease, after life's care and sorrows, the comfort and sweetness of peace.

It's getting dark, but I see light above the city and stars in the sky. I'm thinking about Stein, but mostly I'm thinking about Laika. They called her Little Curly and Little Bug and Little Lemon, and stuck her in a spaceship that wasn't made to come back. Now it's all so easy, all you have to do to get launched into space is come up with a good slogan for chocolate, and I've read that traveling in space means you'll be younger when you return than you would've been had you stayed on earth, because time is relative. A day with Epsilon, for example, isn't the same as a day without.

I've knitted myself a hat, it's plum red with an appealing lace pattern, I figured that a few air holes would be
nice now that it's spring. I put it on and feel like a cranberry
in the snow, and I wonder if they can see me from the moon.
Me and the Great Wall.

Our first meeting with the new neighbors surpassed our expectations. But then I ran into June's mother alone, and there
was something awkward about it, even though I couldn't put
my finger on exactly what. I figured I should say hello, since
I wanted to seem friendly. We were going to be living side by
side, after all, with only a thin wall between us. I expected her
to say hello back, and then we'd each go our own way, and
I got nervous when it looked like she had something else to
say. I watched her patiently for what seemed an eternity, until she finally asked about my sprain, though I'd told her the

day before that it was a chronic pain. That rhymes. So I put my hand on the thigh opposite the one she'd pointed to and leaned forward. I thought it would be good to whisper the secret in her ear, because that would forge a bond between us. I stopped in mid-motion, so she could lean forward and meet me halfway. She seemed a little reluctant, but I tried not to take it personally. I lowered my voice in case anyone was listening. "I think maybe it might be something . . ." Shy, I paused a second before I whispered as low as I could: "Psychological." She didn't say anything, just looked at me like I'd told a lewd joke. Her odd smile felt like a trap. I tried to think of some way out, to come up with something else to talk about, and I looked around. I didn't have to look far. "On the subject of the psyche," I said, relieved at having managed such a painless transition to this new and safer topic. I nodded toward the neighbor's door across the hall: "Did you know he's schizophrenic?" "No he's not," she said. "Oh, but he is," I said, "I've heard several different voices coming from his apartment."

In the store, I look long and hard before I find jam in a tube, I just saw a commercial for it on TV. No one asks me if I need assistance. Being visible from the moon probably wouldn't make a difference in situations like this. When I finally find the right shelf, I think I might as well get two tubes at once. Then I look over my shoulder before putting one under each arm. On my way to the cashier, I think, *My God, where will this end?*

Without thinking about it, I walk up to the register where the girl is sitting, she licks a finger and turns a page in her magazine. My pulse pounds in my temples, my shoes creak on the floor, and a timid old voice whispers in Swedish, "Good morning." I realize it's me.

The girl doesn't answer, and before I know it I've walked right by her. No alarms go off, everything's normal outside, everyone acts like nothing happened. On my way across the parking lot, I can't help but look down on the mothers with strollers, and I snub the doves right to their little bird faces.

Åge B. is in position in the woods, and the banana is back as well. The man is a mystery. It would've made more sense if he was a flasher. Why is he always standing there on the side of the path? It's not completely safe out here, it's infested with ticks, not to mention all the lonely people. But maybe he knows something I don't. He doesn't notice me before I say, "Here I am," and even then he has to look around before he finally sees me. I wait for him to compliment me on my hat, but he just asks for the time. So, I don't get to say any of the things I could've said. I feel incredibly tired. But it's not Åge B.'s fault, and so I give him the time of day.

When I get home, I end up eating slices of bread and straw-berry jam without strawberries, since all that squirts out of the tube is a runny, ugly stream. But I try to be content. If you're content with yourself, God and man have no choice but to be content with you. I realize I don't need a trip around the world or a big career, and suddenly I'm not heavy as lead anymore. Now I'm more like silver. And silver is quite valuable.

"You're a winner," I said to Epsilon, he just looked so depressed. "And they know it." I dropped the last sheet in the laundry basket and fastened a clothespin to one of his shirtsleeves. "They know you're way too smart for the position. The work wouldn't challenge you, you'd get bored, you'd probably quit, and then they couldn't offer you an even better position than the one that's free now." "I'm not that sharp anymore," Epsilon said. "My memory's going." I straightened the part in his hair. "Remember, you taught me everything I know," I said. But Epsilon looked just as sad as ever. "Who do I ask every time I wonder how many sides a right-angled triangle has?" I said. Epsilon smiled a little and picked up the basket. "It's you I ask," I said and threaded my arms through his, although his were full of clothespins. "By the way, you're very handsome." And I wasn't just being nice. I meant it.

There's a program about language on TV and their guest is a man who's nationally renowned for his skill in talking backward. It began with "dog" when he was six years old, and after that nothing could stop him. The host asks if the man could give everyone a little demonstration and the national champion says of course. "We'll begin with a word that's not too long," the host says, "namely, the word *palindromes.*" A few unintelligible sounds rattle out of the national champion's mouth, I'm impressed by how quickly it happens. "And since we're on TV," the host says, "we can play what you've just heard in reverse and find out if he really said *palindromes.*" But it sounds like something completely different. The host looks embarrassed, but the national champion seems happy as ever.

I get up from the chair and go into the bathroom. I take out a new roll of toilet paper and make a perfect start, there's not a single tear in the first sheet. Though I feel nothing but emptiness as I stare at the bathroom floor with a roll of toilet paper in my hand and a German poem stuck in my head.

> Ich weiß nicht, was soll es bedeuten
> Daß ich so traurig bin;
> Ein Märchen aus alten Zeiten,
> Das kommt mir nicht aus dem Sinn.

"MATHEMATICAL PROOFS DON'T just tell you *that* something is true, they also tell you *why* it's true," Epsilon said. I didn't want to listen to him. "Mathea," he'd said when he came in the door, and there was something odd about the way he said my name, as if he'd just repeated it several times. "Please sit at the kitchen table," he continued, in the same mechanical way, and I began to tremble all over, because I was sitting there already. "You know I don't understand any of this," I said, looking at the two circles he'd drawn on a piece of paper in front of him. "It's not as scary as you think," Epsilon said. "It's just systematized common sense." "Epsilon," I said. But he interrupted me: "All you need to do is start with something you already know and draw a chain of logical conclusions to something you want to prove. Every single link in the chain ought to be clear enough that anyone can see that it's correct."

It had happened gradually, starting with the day June was drafted into the military. His father and the accountant were fine with the change, but his mother was suddenly alone in the apartment with no one to do the shopping for her. "She has to eat," Epsilon said. "But there's no hurry," I said, "a human being can go for weeks without food, as long as she gets water, and she has the faucet." Epsilon didn't seem convinced. "Besides, I don't know what she likes," I said. "You can ask her for a shopping list," he said. "Absolutely not, that's crossing the line," I said. And I didn't think anything more of it.

It was several weeks later. Epsilon wasn't home. "What in the world is there to do at work on a Saturday?" I'd asked. "Someone might need me," he'd said, as if I didn't. The plans I'd made for us were down the drain, so I had to be spontaneous. I knew more people would be out than on a weekday, but nonetheless something told me to go to the store. With a feeling of foreboding, I found my net bag. Suddenly, an absurd thought struck me, that I would bump into June's mother. I quickly crossed myself. What would I say to her after all these years?

However, it wasn't June's mother I came upon. It was Epsilon. He knew I didn't shop on weekends. He was standing in the canned-food aisle, not expecting I'd see him standing there wondering what June's mother liked. He had no idea that I flinched at the sight of his back, put my basket down, turned around, and left, all the while wondering if he'd been to work at all.

At home I picked up my knitting project and waited. There are so many sounds in our building, I could hear the water rushing through pipes next door. However, the more I tried to keep from listening, the more I swore I could hear Epsilon's voice. I decided that I had to do something, find a solution, and when Epsilon finally showed up an earwarmer-and-a-half later, I'd already figured out the whole conversation.

"We can move if you really want to," I said. "I don't want to move," Epsilon said. That threw a wrench into my calculations. "But I refuse to move to Svalbard," I said, which was also taking the conversation in a different direction from what I'd originally planned. "The polar bears there are very sly," I continued. "They're all white, just like the snow." Epsilon rubbed his temples, and I felt myself getting tense. "But their snouts are black, so they hide them with their paws when they're getting close to their prey." "What are you talking about,

Mathea?" Epsilon asked. "Still, I wouldn't really have anything to fear," I said, "because you don't need to be faster than the polar bear. You just need to be faster than your companion." There, let him ponder on that.

One day, Epsilon didn't come home after work. From the kitchen window I'd seen him enter the building, and I'd counted the number of steps he had to take to get to the fourth floor. Finally, I went to the peephole. He was standing right between our door and June's mother's, just staring at the stairs. I threw open the door: "Welcome home."

Epsilon got quieter and quieter, and on his birthday I asked him what he was thinking about. I thought it must be about my homemade pudding, but he said it was the Monty Hall problem. It is based on an American TV show, where the contestants could choose between three doors. Two of the doors had a goat behind them and the third had a car. After the contestant chose a door, the host would open one of the other doors instead, and reveal a goat. The contestant then got to choose whether he wanted to stick with the closed door he'd already chosen, or trade it for the remaining closed door.

I looked at Epsilon in disbelief. "Of course he has to keep the one he chose first," I said. "Actually," Epsilon said, "he should trade. The probability that the contestant chose the right door is 1/3 at the beginning, and then he'd lose if he traded doors. But the probability that he didn't choose the right door the first time is 2/3, and in that case he'd win if he traded doors. Therefore, the contestant should trade, since he has a 2/3 chance of winning." "What do you mean by 'winning'?" I asked. "To choose the car," Epsilon said. "Why?" I said. "Imagine the freedom to go anywhere you want," Epsilon said. "Doesn't he like goats?" I asked. Epsilon looked puzzled. "Everyone likes goats, right?" I added. "Well, maybe," he said. "So the first time he's chosen one of the goats?" I asked. "Well . . ." Epsilon stammered, "probably." "Then he has to keep it," I said. "Otherwise he has no honor." Epsilon's eyes grew distant. "More pudding?" I asked. But he abruptly stood up and left the table, still with his fork in hand. I followed him into the living room, I couldn't stand this any longer. "What's going on with you, Epsilon?" I asked. He stopped. He said he didn't know, and I knew he was lying. We stood facing each other, his eyes met mine before he looked down. "I knew it," I said. "I knew you were lying." Epsilon shook his head. "Yes," he said. "Warum?" I asked. "You make everything so difficult." "I don't know," Epsilon said. "No matter what I do, it's the wrong thing." He wasn't crying, and I didn't understand why. "It hurts so much," he said, but he just seemed cold, I didn't recognize him. He put his forkless hand over his heart: "Here." I rolled my eyes. "And I do things without knowing why I'm doing them," he continued. "But what you do is just making everything worse," I said on the verge of tears. Then I walked up to him, grabbed the fork out of his hands, and threw it as hard as I could against the wall. I just couldn't throw it hard enough. Epsilon looked startled. Then it felt like my body couldn't carry me any longer, my shoulders slumped, my knees bent, I was like a puppet on strings hanging from the ceiling. I began to sob. Epsilon hesitantly lifted his hands, I thought he was going to embrace me. But I guess he didn't have the courage, because he just patted me on the arm: "There-there."

That night I dreamed he said her name, and in a fit of vengeance I called Einar Lunde, "my anchorman." However, the worst thing I dreamed was that I sat in a chair with a doll on my lap and pointed at Einar and said: "Look, Daddy's on TV."

The next day we hardly talked to each other. We'd never fought like that before, and neither of us knew what to do. Soon we were just walking around and past each other. Epsilon mostly sat with his nose in a book, while I looked out the kitchen window and daydreamed that June's mother and Epsilon and I went sledding. At the bottom of the hill, she'd disappear—either through God's will or my own.

The seasons changed and Epsilon started acting stranger and stranger. He told me that June's mother had begun leaving her apartment. "Why?" I asked, realizing I'd have to be extra vigilant at the peephole before doing the same. Epsilon didn't even try to convince me that he'd run into her by chance. "She realizes she wants more out of life," he said. "More than canned food?" I asked, but he didn't take the hint.

What had to happen sooner or later, happened. On the way up from the laundry room I heard steps behind me, and I knew it was June's mother. I wanted to run, but I needed to see her. I stopped, nervous, almost feeling sick as I turned around. She was gorgeous, even more so than I remembered. She seemed very short, standing lower down on the stairs. If she wanted to look me in the eyes, she would have to tilt her head back. I told myself that she wasn't able to. I imagined that in the eighties she'd gotten rear-ended and so had whiplash. And I couldn't talk to her while she was standing there staring at my pockets. So I turned and ran as fast as I could up the stairs, then sneaked in through my door.

The military had made a man out of June. Now he could both make his bed and shoot a person—I could see it in his eyes. His mother had also been completely transformed this past year, during which only one special thing had happened to me, and that was when I dislocated my hip. "Now she's going to take a course," Epsilon said almost proudly, as if it was his doing. "In risk measurement." "But she can't pronounce the letter r," I said. "Yes, isn't it wonderful?" Epsilon said. "She's like a freight train now, nothing can stop her."

Epsilon pointed to the two circles he'd drawn on the sheet of paper, one surrounding the other. "We'll call the big circle E and the little circle M," he said, "and then we can say that M implies E." "Isn't there something of M outside of E?" I asked. Epsilon looked from me to the drawing. "I can't . . . I can't see that," he said, and his voice was so unfamiliar. And then, with an unsteady hand, he began to draw a third circle beside the other two, but I didn't want to see it, so I just studied the M and the E. The third circle was approaching the E and I wanted to ask Epsilon to stop, but knew there was no point. I just stared at the big circle that surrounded the little one, my eyes filled with tears, and it became difficult to see, but then I saw, I understood. "Epsilon," I said, but he didn't stop, he kept drawing the third circle. "Doesn't this also mean," I said, "that not-E also implies not-M?" And there, right before the circles crossed, he stopped.

I DON'T LIFT A FINGER, I've been sitting in the chair for days on end and I hardly pay attention to the two flies mating on my left knee. I'm wearing my hat and mumbling that German poem and I wonder why I'm so "traurig."

I gather all my strength and walk to the bookshelf, where I take out the encyclopedia and turn to *B*, because sometimes clarity in one area can shed light on another. It says that even though the banana plant looks like a tree, it's really just a big plant that has flowers without sex organs and fruit without seeds. Therefore, the banana doesn't undergo fertilization and plays no role in the plant's formation, and when the banana plant has lost its fruit, it dies. It was the meaninglessness of this cycle that made Buddha love the banana plant, which he believed symbolized the hopelessness of all earthly endeavors.

I identify with bananas, for not only am I hunched over, I've also got a flower without sex organs and fruit without seed, and therefore I am, according to Buddha, meaningless. And I also believe Buddha was on to something where the hopelessness of all earthly endeavors is concerned, because I feel hopeless; I stole from the grocery store, gave Åge B. the time, buried a time capsule, baked rolls, turned up the hot plate, tried to plan my own funeral, tried to become a tree, and then the most difficult thing of all—I used the telephone, which was really too much for me—and yet I'm still sitting here in my apartment and I'm just as afraid of living life as I am of dying. And wasn't it Buddha who also said that everything is suffering, and I think that if I'd been religious, I would've been a Buddhist, and if I'd been a fruit, I would've been a banana.

I put down the encyclopedia and go sit at the kitchen table. Hamsun said that *nothing is like being breathed on by a life*, and I wish someone would ring my doorbell, even if they just ran away.

One morning, when June's baby carriage was still on the landing, a couple of young girls rang the doorbell. "Can we watch Niels?" they asked and looked from me to the name on the door. "He's at work," I said. Giggling over their mistake, they looked at the door again. "What about Stein?" they asked. "He's dead," I said.

Another robbery might be nice, so at least when the Norwegian Gallup asked when we'd last had a visitor, I could say it wasn't that long ago at all.

They took the TV and the *Statistical Yearbook for the Kingdom of Norway, First Edition, 1880*, from which, among other things, you could learn that *4,568 insane people had been registered (not including idiots) in that year*. Epsilon and I had been on summer vacation, we came out of the forest singing, but the spell was abruptly broken, because when we got to our door we realized something was wrong. "Someone's broken the lock," Epsilon said. "Someone's taken the TV," I said. "Didn't they see the sign?" Epsilon asked. He'd written "we have an alarm" on a piece of paper, because statistics showed that it isn't the alarm itself that prevents burglary, but rather the illusion of an alarm. "So what if we're not a hundred percent truthful," I'd said when I'd hung Epsilon's note below our welcome sign.

At first it looked like they'd just taken the TV and what little silver we had. "Thank goodness," Epsilon said. "As long as we have each other," I said. However, I looked with fresh eyes at the watercolors I'd painted and the homemade pearl necklace lying on the nightstand. Epsilon was surprisingly calm, but that was before he discovered the empty space on the bookshelf. Despondent, he sank down in the nearest chair. Luckily, whenever I laugh it sounds like I'm crying, so Epsilon never got suspicious.

The robbery was nice. It was something to talk about. I myself talked about it for several years, and when he'd gotten a little distance on things, Epsilon could talk about it too.

Even if I don't have the energy to go out, I can always open the window. I'm painfully aware that the light breeze I feel whenever Åge B. breathes on me is nearly like my breathing on myself, so maybe I should try to *breathe on* people other than Epsilon, because it would be nice to mean something to someone. For me at least. However, I haven't even managed to retrieve the newspaper from the doormat the last few days. The papers are probably piling up, and I wonder how long it'll be before someone thinks I might be dead.

Speaking of which, when I close the window and go into the living room to turn on the TV, I find a man who can talk to the dead. "But where are they exactly?" the host asks him. "Where's the Internet?" the man replies.

Einar Lunde is talking again, about everything that's happened over the last day or so. Then the meteorologist comes on and says that Mary the storm is heading for the coast. It hits me like a fist in the gut. Surely I'm faster than Mary. And then I know what I have to do. There's no way to avoid it. "Mary, Mary, quite contrary," I say and head for the empty bedroom.

I'VE DECIDED TO GO to the get-together at the senior center, it's the final thing on my list. I'll stop at the last station before death, I might be claimed at the Lost and Found, it would kill two birds with one stone. That doesn't rhyme, though one might think that it should. I try to keep my nerves under control. I eat jam straight from the tube and read the obituaries, but my thoughts are elsewhere.

I drag a chair from the kitchen to the bathroom, climb up on it, and stand looking at myself in the mirror for a long time. I feel like something's missing besides the seven teeth.

In the bedroom, I feel around in the sheets and finally I find my tiny mole. I use a little spit to glue it to my face and then I clamber back up on the chair in front of the mirror. I've always wondered why you call them "moles" when they're on your back, but "beauty marks" when they're on your face. Now I know why.

I spray perfume on my body's pulse points before I go and find my hat. Then I pull on my newly knitted jacket. After thinking about it for a minute, I consciously button it crookedly. I feel sly but don't know why. That rhymes. I step over the pile of newspapers on the mat.

I stop at the message board in the foyer and read the flier about the get-together one more time, just in case there's any fine print.

The other old people will probably be young and vivacious, at least compared to me. I might be the oldest of them all. It's rarely good to be the oldest of them all. At least not in the West.

Åge B. still doesn't notice my hat or my new jacket, even though I should be visible from Mars. I watch him and wonder how buses can run, how there can be food at the store, how the evening news is always right on time, how the world seems to get by somehow. I brush off my thoughts and carry on. In front of me, I see the old man with the walker, the one I raced a while back, he's probably on his way to the get-together too. He looks so lonely walking there, much lonelier than me, and much, much smaller, but that might be because he's so far away. I catch up to him. If I walk right behind him, people will think we're together. If I'm lucky, the man with the walker will think so too. I almost believe it myself.

When we get to the senior center, I can't bring myself to open the door for him, there's a fine line between shyness and rudeness. We enter a hall full of hats and "granny carts," and from the doorway in front of us I can hear the sound of raised voices—probably trying to drown out the beeping from all those hearing aids. Even though I'm so tired of green carpet and brown wallpaper, I miss them now, at least I know how to act when I'm home, whereas I have no idea how to act in a room full of people. So I close my eyes and follow the man with the walker. "Look, Rolf's here," someone says. "Sit with us, Rolf," someone else calls. I open my eyes again, he looks so different from when it was just him and his walker. I'm about to turn around, I want to go home and plan my death, but then someone in green pants closes the door behind me. "Go ahead and sit down, the show's starting," she says. Apparently, there was some fine print after all.

There's only one table where nobody's sitting. However, it's full of crocheted toilet-seat covers, small homemade dresses meant to hide bottles, wooden signs painted with the Mountain Code for hikers. I sit there after draping my jacket over the seat in front of me, so it looks like someone else is sitting here too. I wonder what makes Walker Rolf so special.

The "show" turns out to be five Pakistani girls in colorful outfits. They tell us they're from the school next door, and then they put on a cassette and dance to strange music, while the old people clap excitedly. I try to be excited and clap too, but fail miserably at both. The music ends and then a woman says: "Let's give a cheer for the Indians." But the suggestion falls flat.

I want to get up now, I've given it a try and I've experienced Pakistan, and what else can one expect, but then green-clad servers start going from table to table with jelly rolls and juice, and jelly rolls aren't exactly the worst thing in the world. While I sit and wait, I look at the five women at the next table over, they mash their dessert with a fork before putting it in their mouths. If I'd brought the bag full of teeth to lend, I could've made myself some friends. Even though they remind me of some housewives I used to know, I would've liked to approach them, but they talk so loudly and hear so badly, and I talk so softly and am so far away.

Instead, I practice saying thanks for the dessert. If the server says something I don't understand, I can just make the sign of the ox, both to seem friendly and to show that deaf people aren't necessarily dumb. I'll have to cross my fingers that they don't understand sign language and ask what color my ox is and whether it has big horns. I try to look hungry, but when someone finally approaches my table, it's not to give me a piece of cake, but instead to take some plastic containers from underneath the table. "Now it's time for the raffle!" she says loudly. Things are getting out of control.

The old people pass around the containers full of tickets, and they unfold these pink and yellow and blue pieces of paper, which they lay on their tables in front of them— each person has a territory, and some have even put their handbags between them to protect it. I'm mostly focused on how close I'm sitting to the green, pressed pants of the woman running the show. If I just lean a little to the side, I can smell detergent, and I want nothing more than to press my head against this nice fabric and cry, I don't know why. That rhymes. But then the woman announces that the draw is about to begin. "We've all got to focus now." I sit up straight again. The woman picks up an embroidered napkin from the table and shows it to the room. "And the lucky winner is . . ." she says and draws a piece of paper from a bowl, "Z-35, Zimbabwe 35." After a few nerve-wracking seconds, a nearly transparent man gives a soft whoop, and I wonder how someone can celebrate winning an embroidered napkin when they're about to die. "Burkina Faso 45" is called, and so it goes until most of the African continent is covered and all the knickknacks and other useless things have been divvied up. The table in front of me is empty. "Now there's only one prize left," the woman says. My cheeks start to burn, because I think she means me. But then she grabs my jacket and holds it up in front of her. "This jacket is rather special," she says after examining it closely. "It looks like it's made out of earwarmers."

I sink down and down, everything is hazy and close around me, and when I finally surface again and draw a breath to say something, it's already too late. The winning ticket has been claimed. At the same time, a man says that the bathroom door has been locked for half an hour and no one answers when he knocks. "Maybe someone had a heart attack," the woman with the winning ticket says, stuffing my jacket into a plastic bag, and everyone gets excited.

I cross the bridge with a pang in my heart and in my stomach. Missing a meal is always painful, and so is missing a jacket. I realize that the jacket meant more to me than I knew. Then I see Rolf's back. Not again, I think, now that his presence reminds me of my own inadequacy. I also can't help wondering how he's managed to get ahead of me when

I didn't see him leave the get-together. Maybe he simply had to get away, maybe they were about to raffle off his glasses or something.

My legs move faster. I know this is my last chance.

I come up alongside him and summon every latent social instinct I have. "Excuse me, do you have the time?" I ask, but don't get any reaction. I know what I have to do. It's not enough to be Mathea Martinsen. I have to be Einar Lunde, everyone notices Einar Lunde.

I tap Rolf on the shoulder. "Excuse me, I'm from the Norwegian Broadcasting Corporation," I say. "Can I ask you a few questions?"

The walker swerves on the asphalt. "What's this about?" Rolf asks.

I get confused and don't know what to say, and then it hits me that there's no point in trying to make friends with him, because it's Mathea Martinsen who needs a friend, not Einar Lunde. The attention I've now drawn to myself is as meaningless as the life cycle of the banana plant, but since Rolf is looking at me questioningly, I can't just stand here, and the only thing left for Mathea Martinsen to do is to figure out how I'm going to reconcile myself to dying.

I make a fist with my right hand and hold it up, now it looks like a microphone. "Eins, zwei, eins zwei," I say and tap on it with my left index finger. I know that Einar Lunde has a much easier time talking to people than I do, so I clear my throat.

"Have you made peace with death?" I ask and extend the microphone to Rolf.

Rolf looks at me for a long moment and it nearly gets awkward.

"Ah," he says and glances around, probably looking for the hidden camera. "Now I understand."

He leans forward. "When it comes to death, I'm ready and willing," he says laughing into the microphone and accidentally spraying it with saliva.

I dry it with the sleeve of my dress.

"But aren't you afraid?" I ask.

"I'm more afraid of living than dying," he says. "You stop fearing death when you're my age."

I don't ask how old he is, in case he's younger than me.

"To tell you the truth," he continues, "I'm looking forward to giving up. Aside from the basic necessities, I've given away everything I own, and if lightning should strike here and now, I'd shout: Come and get me, I'm ready to go!"

"You might be disappointed," I say. "You're standing next to a lightning rod."

Rolf's eyes wander again, then he clears his throat. "I have to go," he says. "I had to leave the senior center, even though I was having such a good time, to go to a doctor's appointment. They take my blood pressure every week. High blood pressure is life-threatening for us old people, you know."

But all I know is that this day has been too much for me. My "last chance" leaves me behind, and it's just all too much. And I can't cry. So I run. I run as fast as I can, past Rolf, across the bridge, and up the hill toward the woods. All I can see is the grass at my feet, but suddenly there's Åge B. I'd completely forgotten him.

I look at Åge B. and he looks through me to the trees on the other side.

I wait for him to ask. Dark clouds gather overhead, a drop of water hits me in the eye, and all I want is to die laughing. I don't need to laugh. I need to cry. But I can't do that either.

I stand with rain falling on my neck, my dress clinging to my body, and I wonder how close you can come to crying without actually crying.

He doesn't ask me anything.

"I don't think life is any good," I say, and start to walk off.

But then Åge B. says, "Life isn't supposed to be good."

"What?" I ask, stopping mid-stride.

"Who said life's supposed to be good?" but he doesn't say it like it's a question, and he doesn't look at me.

"Isn't life supposed to be good?" I ask, still flabbergasted that he's talking to me.

"No," Åge B. says. "It's supposed to be hard."

"But why?" I ask.

"That's just the way it is," Åge B. says.

"Oh," I say and fall silent.

Even if I haven't managed "good," I've certainly managed "hard." And maybe it's good enough that I've done the best that I could. Maybe at least it's enough.

"Do you feel better?" Åge B. turns his head and looks at me through his wet hair.

"Yes," I say.

"Good," Åge B. says.

"Good," I say.

"Oh, and just so you know," Åge B. says and glances at the lace pattern on my hat, "I can see your skull."

DESPITE THE TERRIBLE THUNDERSTORM and the people making noise outside, I'm asleep as soon as I put my head on the pillow, and when I wake up it's morning.

I get up and bring in the mountain of newspapers from the doormat. The Groruddalen newspaper is lying there with the back page facing up, it says that Caretaker Leif has managed to catapult the co-op to victory in the "Groruddalen's best" contest. And this despite the fact that I've asked God every night to let us come in last. There's going to be an awards ceremony, and Leif is asking the residents to dress in yellow, which is the new co-op color. I think of my apricot wedding dress, it can almost pass for yellow. The awards ceremony is taking place today, there's going to be a band (who likes band music anyway?) and the first hoisting of the building's new yellow flag. We don't even have a flagpole, but I guess Leif hasn't noticed.

I carry the newspapers into the kitchen, dump them on the kitchen table and squint at the sharp light coming from the kitchen window. And then I see it—a flagpole right in the middle of the yard. During the night, they erected a flagpole on the exact spot I buried my time capsule. There's a mound of dirt on one side, and I think of the piece of paper with my telephone number that I put in the box. The only thing I put in the box.

I flip to the obituaries. *The heart that beat so hard for us all, the eyes that gleamed so tender, have stopped and dimmed to the sorrow of all, you'll always be in our memories.* I cross out the last few words and write *"you we'll always remember."*

I see that someone named Al will be buried in the Haugerud cemetery at eleven o'clock. That works fine.

I go to the bathroom to get ready. My wedding dress fits perfectly. The only thing I take with me is the sandwich bag full of teeth. Before I go, I stop and look around the apartment. It could've been worse, I think.

My neighbors are gathering around the flagpole, it's so high there's probably snow on top. They're looking at the sky while they listen to Leif tell them loudly how lightning struck twice, one bolt after the other, and how it rained down wood splinters. I look up and see that the finial is missing, the top of the pole is black and there's a furrow running down the side. I leave the yellow gathering and disappear around the corner of our building. I'm apricot now but I can't think of anything to rhyme with apricot.

I enter the church which looks like a swimming hall. I don't ask for whom the bells toll, they're tolling for me. I sit in the first row, that's a good seat. While the pastor is talking, I realize that the word "burial" can be separated into "bury" and "Al."

A lot of the congregation is crying, and I suspect they're not crying for Al, but for themselves, and because before they know they'll be in Al's situation someday. No one envies Al his situation.

I cry too.

"Niels was taken from us his first day of retirement," the pastor said. "What meaning can we find in that?" He looked out over the pews, there weren't many people there and no one had an answer. I sat in the second row and wondered who Niels was. It didn't feel like the pastor was talking about Epsilon.

The Central Statistics Office had finally said enough was enough, and Epsilon and I were going to be together all day every day. We took a walk in the nice weather. As we were passing the parallel bars, I said that now that the earth was spinning again, I wanted to do the same. "That's crazy, Mathea," Epsilon said. "You're no spring chicken." He didn't know I was just joking. "But the nice thing about retirement is that you can start living life," I said. "I don't remember ever doing anything else," Epsilon said. "So you don't even want to give it a try?" I asked. "No," Epsilon said. "You'll be my hero if you do it," I said and kissed him. "No, stop that," Epsilon said. But I knew he didn't mean it. What he actually meant was "do it more, do it more." So I did it more. "Parallel bars aren't dangerous," I said and quoted his words back to him: "The probability that we're going to die is less than ε, if ε equals a microscopically small quantity." But Epsilon just shook his head. So I took his hand and neither of us said anything else. We turned toward home. I felt the cool spring breeze against my cheek, and the bright sky in my eyes, and then I felt his hand slip out of mine.

"For everything there is a season," the pastor said, "and a time for every matter under heaven: a time to be born, and a time to die; a time to plant, and a time to harvest." It almost felt like I was responsible for ending two lives. Three, counting the orchid.

After the funeral a man approached me, he said he was a colleague of Niels's, and then he handed me a cardboard box. "This was in Niels's locker," he said. "I don't know why he didn't take it with him when he left." The box held all my letters. Most were unopened.

Home again, I lay down on my bed and I wondered what would do away with me. And I wondered if I should have the light off or on. But it wouldn't matter. The man with the scythe would find me and my raisin heart no matter what.

After Al has come, lingered, and departed, I take the teeth and leave.

I walk through the woods, Åge B. is there.

"Excuse me," he says, "do you have the time?"

"I have something for you, Åge B.," I say. "Maybe some-day you'll get tired of asking people for the time, and then it would be good to have a watch of your own."

I take off Epsilon's watch. Surely he wouldn't have minded.

"So," I say, "this watch needs to be wound. If you forget to wind it, it'll stop, and then you'll need to ask someone for the time again. Then again, you can always call Miss Time of Day."

"I read in the newspaper that Miss Time of Day is dead," Åge B. says.

"No?" I say.

"No one called her anymore," Åge B. says.

Well, it happens to the best of us, I think, before I hand Åge B. the watch.

"That's not necessary," he says.

"It's the least I can do," I say.

He takes it.

"Well, thanks," he says.

"You're welcome," I say.

"And Åge B., it could be that you're making life harder for yourself than it has to be. Maybe it would be better to drop the B and just be Åge. Maybe just being Åge is enough."

Åge B. doesn't say anything.

"But you'll figure it out," I say and smile good-bye at him with all my teeth.

Then I head towards Lutvann. The carpet is green, the wallpaper is brown and the ceiling is blue.

I pause on the final hill. I listen to the trees and count "one, two, tree" in honor of them, and then I head down the hill as slowly as I possibly can.

When I reach the water's edge, I kneel in the sand. I open the sandwich bag and empty out the teeth. I remember how sure I was that I'd find a use for them and that they'd have some sort of significance. But sometimes you have to give meaning to meaningless things. That's usually how it is. So I pat the sand flat in front of me, before I start placing the teeth. There aren't quite enough of them, but that's okay. I use five small pebbles and a little grass instead. I dust off my hands, stand up and then read my last word. "Mathea." That's meaning enough.

I look out over the water. In a book I read, a condemned man was asked how he imagined life after death. "A life where I could carry with me the memories from this one," he answered. I think that was well said.

I draw my wedding dress over my head and lay it on the ground beside me. Then I take off my shoes and hose and throw my panties into a bush.

I set my feet on the muddy bottom, the water's cold, and I pull my hat down over my ears. I'm not afraid of dying anymore, I'm just afraid of dying alone, and I've already done that. I move forward with purpose, I don't hesitate. The cold hurts and I begin to swim.

Since I'm so hunched over, I have to turn on my back to keep my head above water. I don't weigh anything at all, and I swim farther out and make big circles with my arms and frog kicks with my legs, infinity plus one is over my head and eternity is below me. Soon I'm too far from shore and even the little islands.

I don't swim much farther. I'm completely still and so is time and everything around me. Above me, all I can see are clouds that look like meringues, and the only sound I can hear is ambulance sirens. This time they're coming for me, and without pausing to take a breath, I turn myself over onto my stomach. I'm under water, and it's dark and clear.

NORWEGIAN LITERATURE SERIES

The Norwegian Literature Series was initiated by the Royal Norwegian Consulate Generals of New York and San Francisco, and the Royal Norwegian Embassy in Washington, D.C., together with NORLA (Norwegian Literature Abroad). Evolving from the relationship begun in 2006 with the publication of Jon Fosse's *Melancholy*, and continued with Stig Sæterbakken's *Siamese* in 2010, this multi-year collaboration with Dalkey Archive Press will enable the publication of major works of Norwegian literature in English translation.

Drawing upon Norway's rich literary tradition, which includes such influential figures as Knut Hamsun and Henrik Ibsen, the Norwegian Literature Series will feature major works from the late modernist period to the present day, from revered figures like Tor Ulven to first novelists like Kjersti A. Skomsvold.

KJERSTI A. SKOMSVOLD was born in 1979 in Oslo. *The Faster I Walk, the Smaller I Am*, her first novel, was the winner of the Tarjei Vesaas First Book Prize in 2009.

KERRI A. PIERCE is the translator of Lars Svendsen's *A Philosophy of Evil*, Mela Hartwig's *Am I a Redundant Human Being?*, and other novels available from Dalkey Archive Press.

PETROS ABATZOGLOU, *What Does Mrs. Freeman Want?*
MICHAL AJVAZ, *The Golden Age.*
The Other City.
PIERRE ALBERT-BIROT, *Grabinoulor.*
YUZ ALESHKOVSKY, *Kangaroo.*
FELIPE ALFAU, *Chromos.*
Locos.
JOÃO ALMINO, *The Book of Emotions.*
IVAN ÂNGELO, *The Celebration.*
The Tower of Glass.
DAVID ANTIN, *Talking.*
ANTÓNIO LOBO ANTUNES, *Knowledge of Hell.*
The Splendor of Portugal.
ALAIN ARIAS-MISSON, *Theatre of Incest.*
IFTIKHAR ARIF AND WAQAS KHWAJA, EDS., *Modern Poetry of Pakistan.*
JOHN ASHBERY AND JAMES SCHUYLER, *A Nest of Ninnies.*
ROBERT ASHLEY, *Perfect Lives.*
GABRIELA AVIGUR-ROTEM, *Heatwave and Crazy Birds.*
HEIMRAD BÄCKER, *transcript.*
DJUNA BARNES, *Ladies Almanack.*
Ryder.
JOHN BARTH, *LETTERS.*
Sabbatical.
DONALD BARTHELME, *The King.*
Paradise.
SVETISLAV BASARA, *Chinese Letter.*
RENÉ BELLETTO, *Dying.*
MARK BINELLI, *Sacco and Vanzetti Must Die!*
ANDREI BITOV, *Pushkin House.*
ANDREJ BLATNIK, *You Do Understand.*
LOUIS PAUL BOON, *Chapel Road.*
My Little War.
Summer in Termuren.
ROGER BOYLAN, *Killoyle.*
IGNÁCIO DE LOYOLA BRANDÃO, *Anonymous Celebrity.*
The Good-Bye Angel.
Teeth under the Sun.
Zero.
BONNIE BREMSER, *Troia: Mexican Memoirs.*
CHRISTINE BROOKE-ROSE, *Amalgamemnon.*
BRIGID BROPHY, *In Transit.*
MEREDITH BROSNAN, *Mr. Dynamite.*
GERALD L. BRUNS, *Modern Poetry and the Idea of Language.*
EVGENY BUNIMOVICH AND J. KATES, EDS., *Contemporary Russian Poetry: An Anthology.*
GABRIELLE BURTON, *Heartbreak Hotel.*
MICHEL BUTOR, *Degrees*
Mobile.
Portrait of the Artist as a Young Ape.
G. CABRERA INFANTE, *Infante's Inferno.*
Three Trapped Tigers.
JULIETA CAMPOS, *The Fear of Losing Eurydice.*
ANNE CARSON, *Eros the Bittersweet.*
ORLY CASTEL-BLOOM, *Dolly City.*
CAMILO JOSÉ CELA, *Christ versus Arizona.*
The Family of Pascual Duarte.
The Hive.
LOUIS-FERDINAND CÉLINE, *Castle to Castle.*
Conversations with Professor Y.
London Bridge.

Normance.
North.
Rigadoon.
HUGO CHARTERIS, *The Tide Is Right.*
JEROME CHARYN, *The Tar Baby.*
ERIC CHEVILLARD, *Demolishing Nisard.*
MARC CHOLODENKO, *Mordechai Schamz.*
JOSHUA COHEN, *Witz.*
EMILY HOLMES COLEMAN, *The Shutter of Snow.*
ROBERT COOVER, *A Night at the Movies.*
STANLEY CRAWFORD, *Log of the S.S. The Mrs Unguentine.*
Some Instructions to My Wife.
ROBERT CREELEY, *Collected Prose.*
RENÉ CREVEL, *Putting My Foot in It.*
RALPH CUSACK, *Cadenza.*
SUSAN DAITCH, *L.C.*
Storytown.
NICHOLAS DELBANCO, *The Count of Concord.*
Sherbrookes.
NIGEL DENNIS, *Cards of Identity.*
PETER DIMOCK, *A Short Rhetoric for Leaving the Family.*
ARIEL DORFMAN, *Konfidenz.*
COLEMAN DOWELL, *The Houses of Children.*
Island People.
Too Much Flesh and Jabez.
ARKADII DRAGOMOSHCHENKO, *Dust.*
RIKKI DUCORNET, *The Complete Butcher's Tales.*
The Fountains of Neptune.
The Jade Cabinet.
The One Marvelous Thing.
Phosphor in Dreamland.
The Stain.
The Word "Desire."
WILLIAM EASTLAKE, *The Bamboo Bed.*
Castle Keep.
Lyric of the Circle Heart.
JEAN ECHENOZ, *Chopin's Move.*
STANLEY ELKIN, *A Bad Man.*
Boswell: A Modern Comedy.
Criers and Kibitzers, Kibitzers and Criers.
The Dick Gibson Show.
The Franchiser.
George Mills.
The Living End.
The MacGuffin.
The Magic Kingdom.
Mrs. Ted Bliss.
The Rabbi of Lud.
Van Gogh's Room at Arles.
FRANÇOIS EMMANUEL, *Invitation to a Voyage.*
ANNIE ERNAUX, *Cleaned Out.*
LAUREN FAIRBANKS, *Muzzle Thyself.*
Sister Carrie.
LESLIE A. FIEDLER, *Love and Death in the American Novel.*
JUAN FILLOY, *Op Oloop.*
GUSTAVE FLAUBERT, *Bouvard and Pécuchet.*
KASS FLEISHER, *Talking out of School.*
FORD MADOX FORD, *The March of Literature.*
JON FOSSE, *Aliss at the Fire.*
Melancholy.
MAX FRISCH, *I'm Not Stiller.*

Man in the Holocene.
CARLOS FUENTES, *Christopher Unborn.*
  Distant Relations.
  Terra Nostra.
  Where the Air Is Clear.
WILLIAM GADDIS, *J R.*
  The Recognitions.
JANICE GALLOWAY, *Foreign Parts.*
  The Trick Is to Keep Breathing.
WILLIAM H. GASS, *Cartesian Sonata and Other Novellas.*
  Finding a Form.
  A Temple of Texts.
  The Tunnel.
  Willie Masters' Lonesome Wife.
GÉRARD GAVARRY, *Hoppla! 1 2 3.*
  Making a Novel.
ETIENNE GILSON,
  The Arts of the Beautiful.
  Forms and Substances in the Arts.
C. S. GISCOMBE, *Giscome Road.*
  Here.
  Prairie Style.
DOUGLAS GLOVER, *Bad News of the Heart.*
  The Enamoured Knight.
WITOLD GOMBROWICZ,
  A Kind of Testament.
KAREN ELIZABETH GORDON,
  The Red Shoes.
GEORGI GOSPODINOV, *Natural Novel.*
JUAN GOYTISOLO, *Count Julian.*
  Exiled from Almost Everywhere.
  Juan the Landless.
  Makbara.
  Marks of Identity.
PATRICK GRAINVILLE, *The Cave of Heaven.*
HENRY GREEN, *Back.*
  Blindness.
  Concluding.
  Doting.
  Nothing.
JACK GREEN, *Fire the Bastards!*
JIŘÍ GRUŠA, *The Questionnaire.*
GABRIEL GUDDING,
  Rhode Island Notebook.
MELA HARTWIG, *Am I a Redundant Human Being?*
JOHN HAWKES, *The Passion Artist.*
  Whistlejacket.
ALEKSANDAR HEMON, ED.,
  Best European Fiction.
AIDAN HIGGINS, *A Bestiary.*
  Balcony of Europe.
  Bornholm Night-Ferry.
  Darkling Plain: Texts for the Air.
  Flotsam and Jetsam.
  Langrishe, Go Down.
  Scenes from a Receding Past.
  Windy Arbours.
KEIZO HINO, *Isle of Dreams.*
KAZUSHI HOSAKA, *Plainsong.*
ALDOUS HUXLEY, *Antic Hay.*
  Crome Yellow.
  Point Counter Point.
  Those Barren Leaves.
  Time Must Have a Stop.
NAOYUKI II, *The Shadow of a Blue Cat.*
MIKHAIL IOSSEL AND JEFF PARKER, EDS.,
  Amerika: Russian Writers View the United States.
DRAGO JANČAR, *The Galley Slave.*
GERT JONKE, *The Distant Sound.*

Geometric Regional Novel.
  Homage to Czerny.
  The System of Vienna.
JACQUES JOUET, *Mountain R.*
  Savage.
  Upstaged.
CHARLES JULIET, *Conversations with Samuel Beckett and Bram van Velde.*
MIEKO KANAI, *The Word Book.*
YORAM KANIUK, *Life on Sandpaper.*
HUGH KENNER, *The Counterfeiters.*
  Flaubert, Joyce and Beckett: The Stoic Comedians.
  Joyce's Voices.
DANILO KIŠ, *Garden, Ashes.*
  A Tomb for Boris Davidovich.
ANITA KONKKA, *A Fool's Paradise.*
GEORGE KONRÁD, *The City Builder.*
TADEUSZ KONWICKI, *A Minor Apocalypse.*
  The Polish Complex.
MENIS KOUMANDAREAS, *Koula.*
ELAINE KRAF, *The Princess of 72nd Street.*
JIM KRUSOE, *Iceland.*
EWA KURYLUK, *Century 21.*
EMILIO LASCANO TEGUI, *On Elegance While Sleeping.*
ERIC LAURRENT, *Do Not Touch.*
HERVÉ LE TELLIER, *The Sextine Chapel.*
  A Thousand Pearls (for a Thousand Pennies)
VIOLETTE LEDUC, *La Bâtarde.*
EDOUARD LEVÉ, *Autoportrait.*
  Suicide.
SUZANNE JILL LEVINE, *The Subversive Scribe: Translating Latin American Fiction.*
DEBORAH LEVY, *Billy and Girl.*
  Pillow Talk in Europe and Other Places.
JOSÉ LEZAMA LIMA, *Paradiso.*
ROSA LIKSOM, *Dark Paradise.*
OSMAN LINS, *Avalovara.*
  The Queen of the Prisons of Greece.
ALF MAC LOCHLAINN,
  The Corpus in the Library.
  Out of Focus.
RON LOEWINSOHN, *Magnetic Field(s).*
MINA LOY, *Stories and Essays of Mina Loy.*
BRIAN LYNCH, *The Winner of Sorrow.*
D. KEITH MANO, *Take Five.*
MICHELINE AHARONIAN MARCOM,
  The Mirror in the Well.
BEN MARCUS,
  The Age of Wire and String.
WALLACE MARKFIELD,
  Teitlebaum's Window.
  To an Early Grave.
DAVID MARKSON, *Reader's Block.*
  Springer's Progress.
  Wittgenstein's Mistress.
CAROLE MASO, *AVA.*
LADISLAV MATEJKA AND KRYSTYNA POMORSKA, EDS.,
  Readings in Russian Poetics: Formalist and Structuralist Views.
HARRY MATHEWS,
  The Case of the Persevering Maltese: Collected Essays.
  Cigarettes.
  The Conversions.
  The Human Country: New and

SELECTED DALKEY ARCHIVE PAPERBACKS